Tales of Times Past

Tales of Times Past

THE FAIRY TALES OF

CHARLES PERRAULT

Edited & translated by
Alex Lubertozzi

Illustrated by Gustave Doré

Top Five Books
Oak Park, Illinois

A TOP FIVE CLASSIC

Published by Top Five Books, LLC
521 Home Avenue
Oak Park, Illinois 60304
www.topfivebooks.com

First published 1697. This translation first published 2020.
All rights reserved. The moral right of the translator has been
asserted. The engraved illustrations that accompany the main
text were created by Gustave Doré for an edition published by
J. Hetzel of Paris in 1862; the illustrations for "The Ridiculous
Wishes" (in the Addendum) were made by Harry Clarke for a
1922 edition published in London by George G. Harrap & Co.

ISBN: 978-1-938938-49-8 (hardcover)

TOP FIVE CLASSICS is a series of illustrated great
works, originally created as ebooks and distributed
at low cost, and now available in select print editions.
For more information on Top Five Classics and to
find out about new releases, please visit our website
at: www.topfivebooks.com/TopFiveClassics.html.

Contents

Tales of Mother Goose—*frontispiece from Perrault's 1695 handwritten manuscript.*

Introduction

AIRY TALES, as most of us have grown up thinking of them, exist in their current form in large part because of one man: Charles Perrault. He wasn't the first to publish a collection of traditional folktales, even though he began the project of doing so—first in verse, then in prose—as far back as 1693. Most prominent before him were two Italians who collected their own versions of folktales as they'd heard them. Giovanni Francesco Straparola published *The Facetious Nights* in 1550–53, and Giambattista Basile published *The Pentameron, or, The Tale of Tales* in 1634–36, both of which were themselves inspired in structure and form by Boccaccio's *Decameron* (ca. 1350). In fact, four of the stories included in this book—"Sleeping Beauty," "Cinderella," "Puss in Boots," and "Donkey-Skin"—appeared in different, though recognizable form in one or both of Straparola's and Basile's collections.

Perrault, a writer and scholar employed in the court of Louis XIV, came of age in the mid-1600s, when the vogue among the upper classes in French salons was to retell and embellish these kinds of "peasant" tales. It was in fact a contemporary of his, Madame d'Aulnoy, a writer who published similar tales the same year Perrault's famous collection came out, who coined the phrase *conte des fées*, or "fairy tale." Yet her tales are hardly remembered, if at all. Nor have the tales invented or retold by the previously mentioned Italians enjoyed the same kind of popular longevity. (Most have never heard of *The Facetious Nights* or *The Pentameron*, and despite its reputation, I doubt many could name even one of the hundred tales in *The Decameron*.)

So why have Perrault's fairy tales—or, more accurately, his versions of them—not only survived but flourished and become archetypes of the Western folk tradition? Three reasons immediately come to mind—his selection of tales, the eloquence and wit of his writing, and his revision and censorship of the texts to improve them as stories and enable them to convey definite moral lessons.

Perrault, who had previously published scholarly and poetical works, began publishing tales in verse in 1691 with his novella "Grisélidis," directly adapted from Boccaccio's hundredth and final tale in *The Decameron* (which Chaucer also co-opted for *The Canterbury Tales* as "The Clerk's Tale") a Job-like story of one woman's forbearance in the face of hardship and humiliation. Drawn from folklore, but lacking any sort of magical element, it was not what we think of as a proper fairy tale. But in 1693, he published another verse narrative, "Les souhaits ridicules" ("The Ridiculous Wishes"), which appeared in the November issue of the magazine *Le Mercure galant*. More fittingly described as a genuine fairy tale (even though the "fairy" is the Roman god Jupiter), it was followed by "Peau d'Ane" ("Donkey-Skin"), another fairy tale in verse. The three stories were published in book form in 1694 as *Grisélidis, nouvelle. Avec le conte de Peau-d'Ane et celui des Souhaits ridicules* (*Grisélidis, a Novella: With the Tale of Donkey-Skin and That of the Ridiculous Wishes*).

In 1695 Perrault hired a copyist to prepare a hand-written manuscript with illustrations titled *Contes de ma mère l'Oye* (*Tales of Mother Goose*), containing five tales—"Sleeping Beauty," "Little Red Riding-Hood," "Bluebeard," "Puss in Boots," and "The Fairies." In 1697 the Parisian publisher Claude Barbin printed an expanded edition of the manuscript titled *Histoires ou contes du temps passé. Avec des moralités* (*Stories or Tales of Times Past: With Morals*) keeping "Tales of Mother Goose" for the frontispiece and containing three additional fairy tales—"Cinderella," "Riquet with the Tuft," and "Little Thumbling."

The opening page of "Sleeping Beauty," from Perrault's 1695 hand-drawn manuscript.

The book, printed in two editions in 1697 (the second with some corrections), created a sensation.

Perrault's selection of stories for his *Histoires ou contes du temps passé* certainly played a role in the popularity of the collection. Five of the eight stories—"Little Red Riding-Hood," "Sleeping Beauty," "Cinderella," "Puss in Boots," and "Bluebeard"—would become and remain to this day instantly recognizable titles. And the stories are wonderfully varied, balancing lightness and darkness in subject matter, featuring at different times humor, horror, pathos, and romance. Of course, as I noted earlier, at least half of the stories had had similar versions published elsewhere over the years. On the one hand, it speaks to the wisdom of including tales that are tried and true and that have survived the test of time (and repetition). On the other, it speaks to the obvious fact that Perrault had accomplished something new in his retelling.

Influenced by the rich written tradition going back to Æsop's fables and up through the Italian literary tales (*fabula*), as well as the oral tradition he grew up with and the new fashion of reciting tales in the courtly world of Louis XIV's France, Perrault brought a sophistication and elegance to these humble peasant tales. Updating the tales in some cases to reflect the trappings of contemporary French bourgeois society, he made the stories connect with readers of his day while maintaining their anachronistic charms. Perhaps most winningly is Perrault's humor, sprinkled throughout to great effect and at times distancing the reader from some of the more horrific aspects of the action. In "Little Thumbling," we're told in deadpan style that the Ogre's wife wants to save him because, "even though her man was an Ogre who devoured little children, he was by no means a bad husband." And in the light romp "Puss in Boots," Perrault injects humor by adding the suggestion of something more sinister, as Puss informs the credulous peasants of the absurdly grisly consequences of not doing what he tells them to.

At the same time Perrault keeps the elements that inspire many to refer to fairy tales with the perhaps more apt term "wonder tales." Magical beings—fairies, ogres, talking animals—and enchanted places and objects exist side by side in a recognizable world of princesses and princes, castles and balls, forests, wood-cutters and millers, court intrigue, commerce, and war.

Among the handful of French writers at the time who put their hand to the relatively new genre of fairy tales, Perrault more than any other combined sophisti-cation and humor with an orientation toward reason, a morality that prefigured Enlightenment logic.

In retelling traditional tales, Perrault made sense of stories that lacked sense and created lessons where none existed, or which seemed to impart bad lessons—evil behavior rewarded. Consider the aforementioned precursor to "Sleeping Beauty," Basile's "Sun, Moon, and Talia" from his *Pentameron*. Although similar in structure, the prince who comes to waken Sleeping Beauty (Talia) is no prince, but an already married king. Unable to wake Talia, the king is likewise unable to resist raping the unconscious girl. When she awak-ens later after having given birth to twins (Sun and Moon), the king's betrayed wife tries to exact revenge by eating the children and killing Talia. But the queen is thwarted by the king and a sympathetic cook, and the king and Talia live happily ever after. If that sounds like a story that imparts a confused and depraved lesson, Perrault no doubt agreed, and edited it accordingly.

It's not the approach the Brothers Grimm would take more than a century later when compiling their *Märchen* (see, for example, "The Frog King")—and their fidelity to the oral tradition in documenting it was hugely important. But Perrault's concern in his *Histoires ou contes*, unlike the Grimms, was not anthropological. A scientific approach to retelling folktales reveals more ancient, perhaps meaner and certainly less-reasoned moral values—the insights gleaned from the cultures from which they sprang make them more interesting from a meta perspective (if perhaps less satisfying as stories) and of obvious scholarly value.

None of which is to suggest that all of Perrault's moral lessons hold up after more than three hundred years—particularly in regard to gender roles, perhaps best exemplified by the moral from "Bluebeard," which seems to blame the would-be victim of a serial-murdering husband for her excessive curiosity. Still, Bluebeard is punished for his misdeeds in the end.

In fact, only two of the tales in this collection do not feature happy endings—"The Ridiculous Wishes" (which has a neutral ending) and "Little Red Riding-Hood." In Perrault's retelling, it is a simple warning to children not to talk to strangers (though from the text critics and scholars have derived all sorts of interesting meanings, from the insightful to the truly bonkers). Can it be happenstance that to this day we describe adults who target children as *predators* who *prey* on children? The identification of the storybook Wolf with this form of human violence seems natural but may have its origins in this often retold, revised, and ancient tale. Without Little Red Riding-Hood's death in the jaws of the Wolf (which was undone in later versions to allow for a magical happy ending), the warning does lose some of its "bite." What Perrault is doing in all of his retellings is trying to craft more satisfying stories. Stories in which good is rewarded, evil punished, and careless actions produce predictable results are simply more satisfying to a wider audience than ones in which random consequences are visited on characters good, bad, or careless by an indifferent universe.

So, by carefully selecting his tales; retelling them with style, sophistication, contemporary touches, and humor; and revising them to fit within a rational, "enlightened" moral framework, Perrault helped define what a fairy tale was and would become. In fact, it could be argued he influenced folklore traditions going forward as much as, if not more than, he had been influenced by them.

This is what makes Perrault's fairy tales so signifi-
cant and so worthy of translating anew. Throughout the
eighteenth and nineteenth centuries, writers continued
to build on the fairy tale genre Perrault innovated. The
first European edition of *One Thousand and One Nights*,
translated into French by Antoine Galland, came out in
1704–1717, and Jeanne-Marie LePrince de Beaumont's
shortened version of "Beauty and the Beast" (1756)
remains the standard. The Brothers Grimm collected
more than two hundred of their *Household Tales* in 1812
(substantially revised in 1857), making a lasting impact
to the European folklore tradition in the breadth of
their stories and fidelity to their sources. And in the late
nineteenth century, Scotsman Andrew Lang gathered
together folk and fairy tales from all over the world
beginning with *The Blue Fairy Book* (1889) and continuing on with two dozen more *Fairy Books*. And yet
people continue to return to Perrault's handful of fairy
tales, as Walt Disney did during the twentieth century
when creating animated versions of *Cinderella* and
Sleeping Beauty.

Before Disney, however, the great French artist
Gustave Doré created forty-one unforgettable illustrations for a book of Perrault's fairy tales (*Les Contes de
Perrault*) published 1862 in Paris by J. Hetzel, and which
are included in this edition. In this new translation of
his tales, I have collected all ten of what I consider to be

Perrault's fairy tales—the eight stories that originally appeared in his 1697 *Histoires ou contes*, plus "Donkey-Skin" and "The Ridiculous Wishes." Because the Doré edition included nine tales (the original eight plus "Donkey-Skin"), I have included them here in the order they appeared in the 1862 book. Although the prose version of "Donkey-Skin" was adapted from Perrault's verse tale by an anonymous French author in 1781, it makes only slight variations to Perrault's 1694 version, and I've included it here in part because Doré's illustrations wouldn't quite make sense without the 1781 revisions. I've also added "The Ridiculous Wishes" as an addendum, illustrated by the Irish illustrator Harry Clarke for an English edition put out in 1922.

In various editions of Perrault's fairy tales, including the edition for which Doré created his marvelous engravings, the morals (*moralités*) were often omitted, though the rhyming verses are charming in their original French. I have tried to come closer to Perrault's literal meaning than other translations have done, which are frequently burdened by their own anachronisms, while putting them in modern English and also maintaining some semblance of rhyme and meter.

Some notes on my translation: "Little Red Riding-Hood" is a loose translation of the French title "Le Petit Chaperon Rouge," namely the word *chaperon*, which in those days could refer to a velvet headdress or a velvet band added to a bonnet, or a hood (in falconry). And, although Little Red never goes riding, it seems silly to go against tradition. On the *galette* that Red takes to her grandmother, I decided to stick with the French pastry as Perrault had it. It's been translated over the years variously as a "girdle-cake," "custard," "cakes," and even "round, flat biscuits," which testifies to its inability to be easily translated into English. But the fact that galettes (a category of French pastry most commonly made up of a simple crust wrapped partway over a fruit or savory filling and baked) are no longer so uncommon in English-speaking parts of the world renders such inexact translations unnecessary.

"Little Thumbling" is almost a literal translation of "Le Petit Poucet" (minus the article *le*)—the French for thumb being *pouce*, with the added *t* a diminutive suffix. More often, the title and character have been changed to "Hop o' My Thumb," an anachronistic term for a little person, or sometimes "Tom Thumb," which is confusing as Tom is the eponymous character from the first English fairy tale, published in 1621, who remains thumb-sized his whole life and goes through quite different adventures than Little Thumbling.

"Cinderella" owes its name to the first English translation of Perrault's fairy tales by Robert Samber in 1727, who changed "Cendrillon" (a play on the French word for cinder or ash, *cendre*, which was in turn a play on the Italian word for cinder, *cenere*, used in Basile's tale "Cenerentola") to Cinderilla. Her name took on the more English-sounding suffix "-ella" in an 1804 translation published by Tabart & Co. in London, and it hasn't changed since (although a few have tried, notably Christine A. Jones, who rendered her name as "Ashkins" in 2016). Likewise, in the story, the more vulgar nickname for Cinderella is, in the French, *Cucendron*, which prefixes the word *cul*, French slang for "ass," to *cendre*, which I've rendered as the appropriately childish, though slightly less vulgar, "Cinder-butt."

"Puss in Boots" was originally "Le Maître Chat, ou, Le Chat Botté" (literally "The Master Cat, or, The Booted Cat"), but like some of the other loose translations, "Puss in Boots" has a charm only exceeded by its familiarity. In other places, I've tried to maintain some of the Frenchness of the original, as in the minute detail of the exact type of gold coins—*écus au soleil* and *Louis d'ors*—that the Donkey in "Donkey-Skin," um, "leaves" in his stable each morning.

In every other way, I've attempted to retain the charm, wonder, and simple yet elegant language of Perrault's original tales, rendered in a modern and hopefully timeless new English translation.

Alex Lubertozzi

Tales of Times Past

Passing through a wood, she encountered the Wolf.

Little Red Riding-Hood

NCE upon a time in a small village there lived a little girl, the prettiest anyone had ever seen. Her mother was crazy about her, and her grandmother was even more so. The girl's good mother had had a little red cloak made for her, and it suited the girl so well that everybody called her Little Red Riding-Hood.

One day, her mother, having baked some galettes, said to her, "Go, my dear, and see how your grandma is doing, for I hear she has been ill. Bring her a galette and this little pot of butter."

Little Red Riding-Hood left right away to go to her grandmother, who lived in another village. Passing through a wood, she encountered the local Wolf, who had a mind to eat her up, but he dared not, because of some woodcutters about in the forest.

He asked her where she was going. The poor child, who did not know that it was dangerous to stop and talk to a wolf, said to him, "I am going to see my grandmother and bring her a galette and a little pot of butter from my mother."

"Does she live far off?" said the Wolf.

"Oh, yes," said Little Red Riding-Hood, "beyond that mill you see there, at the first house in the village."

"Well," said the Wolf, "I want to go and see her too. I'll take this path here, and you take that one, and we'll see who gets there first."

The Wolf set off running as fast as he could, taking the shorter path, while the little girl went by the longer path, distracting herself by gathering hazelnuts, chasing after butterflies, and making bouquets of the little flowers she found. It wasn't long before the Wolf got to her grandmother's house. He rapped on her door, *knock, knock.*

"Who's there?"

"It's your granddaughter, Little Red Riding-Hood," said the Wolf, imitating her voice, "and I've brought you a galette and a little pot of butter, which my mother sent you."

The good grandmother, who was in bed because she was still a little sick, called out, "Pull the peg, and the latch will open."

The Wolf pulled the peg, and the door opened. He fell upon the good woman and devoured her in less than an instant, as it had been more than three days since

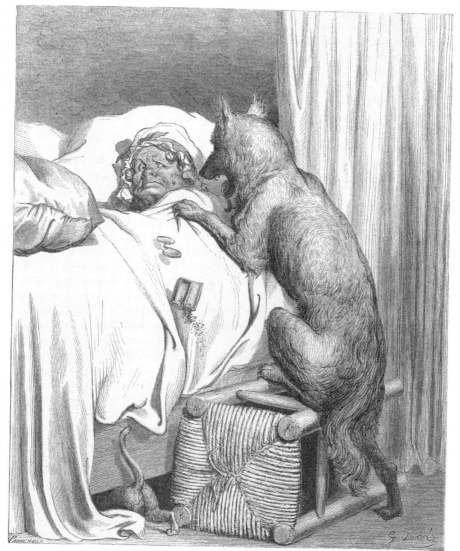

The Wolf fell upon the good woman and devoured her.

he had eaten. Then he shut the door, climbed into the grandmother's bed, and waited for Little Red Riding-Hood. She arrived a short time later and rapped on the door, *knock, knock.*

"Who's there?"

Little Red Riding-Hood, who could hear the deep voice of the Wolf, was afraid at first. But believing that her grandmother was hoarse from a cold, answered, "It's your granddaughter, Little Red Riding-Hood, and I've brought you a galette and a little pot of butter, which my mother sent you."

The Wolf called out to her, softening his voice as much as he could, "Pull the peg, and the latch will open."

Little Red Riding-Hood pulled the peg, and the door opened. The Wolf, hiding in the bed under the blanket, saw her come in and said to her, "Put the galette and the little pot of butter on the sideboard, and come to bed with me."

Little Red Riding-Hood undressed and went into the bed, where she was shocked to see how her grandmother looked in her nightgown. She said to her, "Grandma, what great big arms you have!"

"The better to hug you with, my dear."

"Grandma, what great big legs you have!"

"The better to run with, my child."

"Grandma, what great big ears you have!"

She was shocked to see how her grandmother looked in her nightgown.

"The better to hear you with, my child."

"Grandma, what great big eyes you have!"

"The better to see you with, my child."

"Grandma, what great big teeth you have!"

"The better to eat you with!"

And, saying these words, the wicked Wolf fell upon poor Little Red Riding-Hood and ate her all up.

THE **M**ORAL.

Children, girls most of all—so sweet,
So pretty, so innocent and nice—
Don't listen to everyone you meet;
But if you do, don't be surprised,
When it's you the wolf means to eat.

I say wolf, as there are many kinds:
Some seem mild-mannered, benign,
Without wrath—smooth and refined—
Who follow girls from time to time,
These wolves are the most dangerous kind!

Little Thumbling

NCE upon a time there lived a woodcutter and his wife, who had seven children, all boys. The eldest was only ten years old, and the youngest was seven. People were amazed that the woodcutter could have had so many children in such a short time, but his wife went about her duties efficiently and never had less than two at a time.

They were very poor, and their seven children were a great burden on them, for none of them could yet earn his own living. What grieved them more was that the youngest was very delicate and did not speak a word—what they took for dull-wittedness was in fact a mark of good sense.

This youngest boy was very small, and when he came into the world, he was hardly bigger than a man's thumb, and so he was called "Little Thumbling." The poor child was the scapegoat of the family, and they

"You must see that we can no longer feed our children."

always blamed him for everything. However, he was the finest and most astute of all his brothers, and if he spoke only a little, he listened a great deal.

Then came a very unhappy year, when the famine was so great that these poor people resolved to get rid of their children. One evening, after the children had gone to bed, the woodcutter was sitting with his wife by the fire, his heart aching with sorrow, and he said to her, "You must see that we can no longer feed our children. I cannot watch them starve to death before my eyes. I have decided to take them into the woods tomorrow and lose them there. It will be easy enough, for while they are occupying themselves with gathering kindling, we only need to run away without their seeing us."

"Ah!" cried the woodcutter's wife, "do you mean to tell me you could abandon your own children?"

Though her husband dutifully reminded her of their terrible poverty, she could not bear the thought of it. She was poor, but she was their mother. In the end, however, having considered what pain it would cause her to see them die of hunger, she consented to the plan, and went to bed in tears.

Little Thumbling had heard everything they said. Having overheard from his bed that they were having a serious conversation, he had gotten quietly out from under his covers and slipped under his father's stool so that he could listen without being seen. After going back to bed again, he did not sleep a wink for the rest of the night, thinking about what he ought to do. He rose early the next morning and went to the edge of a stream. There he filled his pockets with little white pebbles and came quickly back home.

They all set out, and Little Thumbling revealed nothing of what he knew to his brothers.

They went into a forest that was so thick they couldn't see each other even ten paces apart. The woodcutter began to chop wood, and the children began to collect bundles of twigs. Seeing them busy at their task, the father and mother gradually inched away from them, and then furtively hurried off down a small, roundabout path.

When the children found themselves alone, they started to cry and scream with all their might. Little Thumbling let them cry, knowing well the way he would get back home again. For on the way there, he had dropped the little white pebbles that he had in his pocket all along the path.

"Don't be afraid, brothers," he then said. "Father and Mother have left us here, but I will bring you back home. Just follow me."

They fell in behind him, and he led them straight to their house by the same path that they had taken into the forest. They dared not enter at first but stood against

Little Thumbling rose early the next morning and went to the edge of a stream. There he filled his pockets with little white pebbles.

*When the children found themselves alone, they started
to cry and scream with all their might.*

On the way there, he had dropped the little white pebbles
that he had in his pocket all along the path.

the door to listen to what their father and mother were saying.

Now it happened that, as soon as the woodcutter and his wife had arrived home, the lord of the manor sent them ten crowns that he had owed them for a long time, and which they had given up hope of ever seeing. This gave them new life, for the poor people were starving.

The woodcutter sent his wife off to the butcher shop at once, and as it had been such a long time since they had had anything to eat, she bought three times as much meat as a supper for two required.

When they were well stuffed with food, the woodcutter's wife began to lament. "Alas!" she said, "where our poor children are now, they could make a feast off what we have left! Mind you, William, it was you who wanted to lose them. I told you that we would regret it. What are they doing now in that forest? My God, wolves may have already devoured them! You must be a monster to forsake your own children this way!"

At last the woodcutter lost his patience, for she repeated more than twenty times that he would regret it, and that she had said so. He threatened to beat her if she did not hold her tongue. The woodcutter was perhaps no more upset than his wife, but she browbeat him. And, like many men, he preferred a woman who always said the right thing to one who was always in the right.

"Alas!' cried the woodcutter's wife, bursting into tears, "where are my children now, my poor children?"

She said it once so loudly that the children at the door heard it plainly. Together they all shouted out, "Here we are! Here we are!"

She ran to open the door for them and cried as she kissed them, "How glad I am to see you again, my dear children! You must be very weary and no doubt hungry. And you, Peter, how filthy you are—come and let me wash you!" Peter was her eldest son, whom she loved more than all the others because he was a little redheaded, and she was also a little redheaded.

They sat down at the table and ate with an appetite that pleased their father and mother. The boys all spoke at once, as they recounted the fear they had felt in the forest.

These good folks were delighted to have their children back with them, and their joy continued as long as the ten crowns lasted. But when the money was spent, they fell back into their former sorrow. Once again they resolved to be rid of their children. They would lead them much further into the forest than the first time and do the job right. They could not manage to speak of this so quietly or secretly, however, that Little Thumbling did not hear them.

Little Thumbling resolved to do as he had done before, but when he got up early in the morning to go

They ate with an appetite that pleased their father and mother.

out and collect his pebbles, he found the door of the house doubly locked, so he could not carry out his plan. He didn't know what to do until the woodcutter's wife gave them each a morsel of bread for their breakfast. He realized he could use the bread in place of the pebbles, throwing his crumbs along the path they took, and so he tucked the bread into his pocket.

Their father and mother led them into the thickest and darkest corner of the forest, and as soon as they

were there, employed a ruse to slip away and leave
the children all alone. Little Thumbling wasn't much
bothered by this, as he believed he could easily discover his way home by the crumbs he had scattered
wherever he had gone. But, to his dismay, he did not
find a single crumb—birds had swooped down and
eaten them all.

Now they were in dire distress, for every step they
took led them deeper into the forest and only got them
more lost. Night came, and a terrible wind blew, which
filled them with dread. On every side they seemed
to hear nothing but the howling of wolves that were
coming to eat them. They hardly dared to speak or
turn their heads. Then it began to rain so heavily that
they were soon soaked to the bone. At every step they
tripped and fell in the muck, getting up all muddy and
not knowing what to do with themselves.

Little Thumbling climbed to the top of a tree to
find out if he could see anything. Turning his head
all round, he spied a small glimmer like the light of a
candle, far away beyond the forest. He climbed down
from the tree, but was disappointed to find that from
the ground he could see nothing of it.

Having walked for some time in the direction of
the light, however, he caught a glimpse of it again as
they were nearing the edge of the forest. At last they
arrived at the house where the candle was burning, but

*Little Thumbling climbed to the top of a tree to find out
if he could see anything.*

not without some anxious moments, for every time they went down into a valley they lost sight of it.

They knocked at the door, and a good woman opened it to them. She asked what they wanted. Little Thumbling explained that they were poor children who had lost their way in the forest, and he begged her, for charity's sake, to give them a place to sleep.

Seeing how adorable they all were, the woman began to cry and said to them, "Oh, you poor little dears, where did you come from? Do you not know that this is the house of an Ogre who eats little children?"

"Alas, madam!" replied Little Thumbling, trembling with fear and cold like the rest of his brothers, "what shall we do? The wolves of the forest are certain to devour us tonight if you do not take us in. And, that being the case, we would prefer to be eaten by your husband. Perhaps he will take pity on us, if you plead for us."

The Ogre's wife, thinking she might be able to hide them from her husband till the next morning, let them in and set them to warm beside a nice fire, where a whole sheep was cooking on the spit for the Ogre's supper. But just as they had started to get warm, they heard three or four great knocks at the door. The Ogre had returned. So his wife hid them quickly under the bed and hurried to open the door.

A good woman opened the door to them.

The Ogre asked if his supper was ready and if the wine were opened, and then immediately sat down at the table. The sheep was still bloody, but it seemed all the better to him for that. He sniffed to the right and to the left and said he could smell fresh flesh.

"It must be this calf," his wife said, "which I have just dressed, that you smell."

"I smell fresh flesh, I tell you," replied the Ogre, eyeing his wife askance and adding, "There is something going on here that I do not understand." Saying these words, he rose up from the table and went straight over to the bed. "Aha!" he said, "so this is how you deceive me, you cursed woman! I don't know why I don't eat you too—it's just as well that you're a tough old beast. Here is prey that comes to me willingly, a tasty treat for my three ogre friends who will be coming to visit in a few days."

Then he dragged the boys out from under the bed, one after another. The poor children dropped to their knees and begged him for mercy, but they were dealing with the cruelest of ogres. Far from pitying them, he was already devouring them with his eyes and telling his wife what delicious morsels they would make with the right sauce.

He went off to retrieve a large knife, which he sharpened on a long stone in his left hand as he drew near the children. He grabbed one of them, and just

"I smell fresh flesh, I tell you," replied the Ogre....
"There is something going on here that I do not understand."

*The Ogre dragged the boys out from under the bed,
one after another.*

then his wife said, "What do you want to do it now for? Won't there be time enough tomorrow?"

"Shut up," said the Ogre. "They won't be as fresh."

"But you have such a lot of meat," replied his wife. "There's a calf, two sheep, and half a pig."

"You're right," said the Ogre. "Give them a good supper to fatten them up, and put them to bed."

The good woman was delighted and brought the children a hearty supper, but the poor wretches were so paralyzed with fear that they couldn't eat a bite. As for the Ogre, he started drinking again, very pleased to have such good entertainment for his friends. He downed a dozen more cups than usual and had to go off to bed early, as all the wine had gone to his head.

Now the Ogre had seven daughters, all still children. These little ogresses had the most lovely complexions, for, like their father, they ate fresh flesh. But they had little round gray eyes, hooked noses, and great big mouths with long, very sharp teeth, set far apart. They were not so wicked just yet, but they showed great promise, for they were already in the habit of biting little children to suck their blood.

They had gone to bed early, and all seven were in a great bed, each with a gold crown upon her head. In the same room was another, equally large bed. Into this the Ogre's wife put the seven little boys, and then went to sleep herself beside her husband.

Little Thumbling was afraid that the Ogre would suddenly regret that he had not cut their throats earlier that evening. Having noticed that the Ogre's daughters all had gold crowns upon their heads, he got up in the middle of the night and softly placed his own cap and those of his brothers on their heads and carefully replaced his own and his brothers' caps with the girls' gold crowns. This way, if the Ogre were to feel like slaughtering them that night, he would mistake his daughters for the boys, and the boys for his daughters.

The thing worked out just as he had anticipated. The Ogre, having awoken at midnight, rued having put off till tomorrow what he could have done that night. Charging out of bed, he seized his big knife and fumed, "Let's go see how the little imps are doing. We won't make the same mistake twice!"

So he groped his way up to his daughters' room and approached the bed where the seven little boys were. All were asleep, except for Little Thumbling, who lay petrified as the Ogre touched the head of each of his brothers in turn and finally touched his own.

"Upon my word," said the Ogre, as he felt Little Thumbling's golden crown, "a pretty job I was going to make of it! I can see I had a little too much to drink last night."

Then he went to the bed where his daughters lay, and here he felt the little boys' caps on their heads.

"Aha, here are the little rascals!" he cried. "Let us work boldly now!"

On saying these words, without a second thought, he cut the throats of his seven daughters. Well pleased with himself and this expedition, he went back to bed beside his wife.

No sooner did Little Thumbling hear the Ogre snoring than he woke up his brothers, urging them to dress quickly and follow him. They crept quietly down to the garden and jumped over the wall. They ran almost all night, racked with fear and without any idea where they were going.

When the Ogre woke up the next morning, he said to his wife, "Go upstairs and dress those little scamps who were here last night."

The Ogre's wife was astonished at her husband's kindness, not suspecting that he meant "dress" in any other way than to put their clothes on. When she went upstairs, however, she was horrified to discover her seven daughters bathed in blood, their throats slashed. She fainted straight away and fell to the floor (which is the first response of most women to such encounters).

The Ogre, fearing his wife was taking too long in carrying out the task he had given her, went up to help. He was no less appalled by the dreadful scene that confronted him than his wife had been. "What's this I have

Without a second thought, he cut the throats of his seven daughters.

done?" he cried. "I will pay those wretches back, and right away!"

He threw a jug of water into his wife's face, and having brought her around, ordered her to fetch his seven-league boots, so that he might overtake the children.

He set off over the countryside and strode far and wide until he came to the road along which the poor children were going. They were only a few hundred yards from their parents' home when they saw the Ogre striding from hilltop to hilltop in his magic boots, stepping over rivers as easily as one would cross the slightest streams.

Little Thumbling spotted a hollowed-out rock nearby and hid his brothers and himself under it, all the while keeping a vigilant eye on wherever the Ogre went.

Now the Ogre was feeling very weary after so much fruitless hiking (for seven-league boots are very tiring to the wearer), and felt like taking a little rest. As luck would have it, he went and sat down on the very rock under which the little boys were hiding. Overcome by exhaustion, it was not long before he fell asleep and began to snore so loudly that the poor children were as frightened as when he had held his great knife to their throats.

Little Thumbling was less afraid. He told his brothers to run home at once, while the Ogre was still sound asleep, and not to worry about him. They took his advice and hurried home. Little Thumbling now approached the sleeping Ogre and gently pulled off his boots, which he immediately put on himself. The boots were very large and very heavy, but being enchanted boots they had the ability to grow larger or smaller

*Little Thumbling now approached the sleeping Ogre
and gently pulled off his boots.*

according to the legs inside them, so they always fit as if they had been made for the feet that wore them.

He went straight to the Ogre's house, where he found the Ogre's wife weeping over her slaughtered daughters. "Your husband is in great danger," Little Thumbling said to her, "for he has been captured by a gang of thieves, and they have sworn to kill him if he does not hand over all his gold and silver. Just as they held a dagger to his throat, he saw me and asked me to come and warn you of his situation to tell you to give me everything of value that he owns, without holding back a thing, or else they will kill him without mercy. As the matter is pressing, he wanted me to wear his seven-league boots, to save time and to prove to you that I am no impostor."

The Ogre's wife, greatly distressed, immediately gave Little Thumbling everything she had, for even though her man was an Ogre who devoured little children, he was by no means a bad husband.

Little Thumbling, laden with all the Ogre's wealth, returned to his parents' home, where he was received with great joy.

. . .

THERE are many who do not agree about this last adventure, and insist that Little Thumbling never committed this theft from the Ogre, and only took the seven-league boots, about which he could feel no remorse, since the Ogre only used them for catching little children. These folks claim that they are in a position to know, having been guests at the woodcutter's cottage. They also say that when Little Thumbling had put on the Ogre's boots, he went off to the court of the

King, where he knew there was much anxiety over the result of a battle that was being fought by the army two hundred leagues away. They say that he went to the King and promised to bring news of the army before the day was out, and that the King agreed to pay him a large sum of money if he could accomplish it.

Little Thumbling brought news that very night, and when this deed was known far and wide, he made as much money as he wanted. For not only did the King pay him handsomely for carrying orders to the army, but many ladies at court paid him to receive news of their lovers, and this was his greatest source of income. He was occasionally entrusted by wives with letters to their husbands, but this paid so poorly, and this branch of the business brought in so little, that he did not even bother to reckon what he made from it.

After acting as courier for some time and amassing great wealth from it, Little Thumbling returned to his parents' house and was greeted there with the greatest joy imaginable. He made all his family well-to-do, buying newly created positions for his father and brothers, and in this way, settled them very handsomely in the world while rising high in the King's favor as well.

THE MORAL.

Over many children we never mourn,
When they are handsome, healthy, and strong;
But when a silent runt happens along,
Don't be hateful, sullen, or forlorn—
For many times it's that small, quiet one,
Who in the end becomes the favorite son.

Sleeping Beauty

NCE upon a time there lived a King and a Queen who were so distraught over the fact that they had no children—they were more distraught than words can tell. They tried the waters of every land, made vows, pilgrimages, and small devotions. They did everything they could do, but nothing worked. Finally, however, the Queen grew large—she was with child—and in due course delivered a baby daughter.

They held a grand christening, and all the fairies that could be found in the realm (there were seven of them) were given to be godmothers to the little Princess. With the gifts that each would bestow upon her in turn—as was the custom of fairies in those days—the Princess would be endowed with every imaginable perfection.

After the baptismal ceremonies, all the guests returned to the King's palace, where a great feast was given in honor of the fairies. Places were laid for them in magnificent style, and each setting's solid gold cover was removed to reveal a golden fork, knife, and spoon, each set with diamonds and rubies. But just as everyone took their places at the table, into the room came an elderly fairy, whom no one had thought to invite as she had not ventured out of her tower in more than fifty years, and they all supposed her to be dead or bewitched.

The King ordered a place to be set for her, but it was impossible to give her a golden setting as they had the other fairies, for only seven had been made. The old creature believed that she was being intentionally slighted, and muttered threats between clenched teeth. One of the young fairies who was seated near her overheard this and, guessing that she might bestow some mischievous gift upon the little Princess, hid behind the tapestry as soon as the guests had left the table. She meant to be the last to approach the Princess, and so be able to counteract, as much as possible, any harm that the old fairy might do.

Then the fairies began to give their gifts to the Princess. The youngest fairy's gift was that the Princess would be the most beautiful person in the world; the next, that she would have the temperament of an angel; the third, that she would do everything with admirable grace; the fourth, that she would dance flawlessly;

the fifth, that she would sing like a nightingale; and the sixth, that she would play every kind of musical instrument with absolute perfection.

The aged fairy's turn now came. Shaking her head, out of spite rather than decrepitude, she declared that the Princess would prick her hand with a spindle, and that she would die of it. This terrible gift sent a shudder through the room, and there was not a dry eye among the company present.

But at that moment the young fairy stepped out from behind the tapestry and said, "Take comfort, my King and Queen, your daughter shall not die. Though my power is not enough to undo all that my aged sister has decreed, the Princess will indeed prick her hand with a spindle. But instead of dying she shall merely fall into a deep sleep that will last one hundred years. At the end of that time, the son of a king shall come to awaken her."

The King, in an attempt to avert the unhappy fate foretold by the old fairy, at once issued an edict forbidding all persons from using a spinning-wheel or keeping a spindle in the house, on pain of death.

After fifteen or sixteen years, with the King and Queen away visiting one of their villas, the young Princess was running about the castle one day, going from room to room and eventually to the top of a tower with a small garret, where an old woman sat alone spinning with her spindle. This good woman had never heard of the King's decree banning the use of spinning-wheels and spindles.

"What are you doing, my good woman?" asked the Princess.

"I am spinning, my beautiful child," replied the woman, not knowing who she was.

"How pretty!" said the Princess. "How do you do it? Let me try and see if I can do it as well as you."

Perhaps because she took up the spindle a bit hastily, and a little carelessly—and maybe because the fairy had foretold it—no sooner had the Princess taken the spindle than it pierced her hand, and she fell to the floor unconscious.

Mortified, the good woman cried out for help. People came running from every corner of the castle. They threw water on her face, soothed her, clapped her hands, rubbed her temples with rosemary perfume, but nothing could restore her.

Then the King, who had returned and rushed upstairs when he heard the commotion, remembered the fairy's prophecy. Deciding that what had happened was inevitable, since the fairies had ordained it, he ordered the Princess to be placed in the finest apartment in the palace, upon a bed embroidered in gold and silver.

*This good woman had never heard of the king's decree
banning the use of spinning-wheels and spindles.*

She looked like an angel, so beautiful she was, even in a trance. Her swoon had not dimmed the bright colors of her complexion: her cheeks were flushed crimson, her lips like coral. Though her eyes were closed, her gentle breathing could be heard, and it was plain that she was not dead. The King commanded that she be allowed to sleep in peace until the time of her awakening should come.

The good fairy who had saved her life by condemning her to sleep a hundred years was in the kingdom of Mataquin, twelve thousand leagues away when the accident happened to the Princess. She was immediately told of it, however, by a little dwarf who wore a pair of seven-league boots (which enable the wearer to cover seven leagues at a single stride). The fairy set off at once, and after an hour her chariot of fire, drawn by dragons, was seen approaching.

The King helped her down from her chariot, and she approved of all that he had done. But having great powers of foresight, she knew that when the Princess awoke, she would be very much confused to find herself all alone in the old castle. So this is what she did: she touched with her wand everybody who was in the castle (except the King and Queen)—governesses, maids of honor, chambermaids, gentlemen, officers, stewards, cooks, dishwashers, errand boys, guards, porters, pages, and footmen. She also touched all the horses in the stables and their grooms; the big mastiff dogs in the courtyard; and little Puff, the pet dog of the Princess, who was lying on the bed beside his mistress. The moment she touched them, they all fell asleep, to awaken only at the same moment as their mistress. Thus they would always be ready to serve her whenever she required it. The very spits before the fire, loaded with partridges and pheasants, subsided into slumber, and the fire as well. All was done in a moment, for the fairies do not dawdle over their work.

Then the King and Queen kissed their beloved child, though it did not wake her, and left the palace. Proclamations were issued, forbidding anyone to approach the palace. But the warnings were unnecessary, for within a quarter of an hour there grew up all around the castle grounds so vast a quantity of large trees and small, with interwoven brambles and thorns, that neither beast nor man could penetrate them. Only the tops of the castle towers could be seen, and then only from a distance. No doubt the fairy had mastered her trade, because the Princess now had nothing at all to fear from curious, prying eyes.

• • •

AFTER a hundred years, the crown had passed to a king from a different family than that of the sleeping Princess. One day his son went hunting near the old palace grounds and, seeing towers peeking out above the trees in a great, dense forest, asked what they were. His attendants related to him the various tales they had heard. Some said there was an old castle haunted by ghosts, others that all the sorcerers in the region held their unholy rites there. The prevailing wisdom was that an ogre lived in the castle, and that he carried all the children he could catch there, then devoured them at his leisure. Since he was the only one who could force a passage through the thick wood, nobody had been able to pursue him.

The Prince scarcely knew which story to believe, when an old peasant spoke up. "Your Highness," he said, "more than fifty years ago I heard my father say that in that castle lies a Princess, the most beautiful in the world, that it is her fate to sleep there for a hundred years, and that she would be awakened by the son of a king, for whom she waits."

This tale fired the young Prince's sense of adventure. Believing he was destined to end the Princess's enchantment, and driven by his desire for love and glory, he resolved at that moment to see what was there. No sooner had he taken a step toward the woods than the giant trees, brambles, and thorns separated, making a path for him. He advanced toward the castle, which he could see at the end of a long corridor. As he walked on, he was surprised to see that the trees closed

*The king's son, seeing towers peeking out above the trees
in a great, dense forest, asked what they were.*

up again as soon as he had passed, so that none of his
entourage could follow him. But a young and amorous
Prince must still be valiant, so he continued on his way,
and soon reached a large forecourt.

The sight that now confronted his eyes was enough
to paralyze him with fear. The silence of the place was
dreadful, and death seemed all about him. The reclining figures of men and animals had all the appearance

43

He advanced toward the castle, which he could see
at the end of a long corridor.

of being dead, until he perceived by the pimply noses and ruddy faces of the porters that they were merely sleeping. It was plain, too, from their half-filled glasses, which still held some dregs of wine, that they had fallen asleep while drinking.

The Prince passed through a large courtyard paved with marble, mounted the staircase, and entered the room of the guards, who were ranged in a line, muskets

The reclining figures of men and animals had all the appearance of being dead.

on their shoulders and snoring their loudest. Crossing through several rooms full of ladies and gentlemen— some on their feet, others seated, but all asleep—he came to a chamber adorned entirely with gold and saw a bed, the curtains of which were open on all sides. Lying on the bed was the most beautiful vision he had ever seen: a Princess, fifteen or sixteen years old, whose transcendent brilliance was something luminous

He crossed through several rooms full of ladies and gentlemen— some on their feet, other seated, but all asleep.

Lying on the bed was the most beautiful vision he had ever seen.

and divine. Trembling with admiration, he approached and knelt beside her.

Then, at that moment, as the end of the enchantment came, the Princess awoke and looked upon the Prince with eyes more tender than a first glance would seem to permit.

"Is it you, my Prince?" she asked. "You have been so long in coming."

The Prince, charmed by her words, and even more by the manner in which she said them, didn't know how to express his own joy and gratitude. He told her that he loved her more than he did himself, and though he fumbled for the words, they pleased her all the more—after all, the less the eloquence, the more the love.

He was more embarrassed than she was, and it should not surprise us, as she had had more time to think about what she would say to him. It seems (though history says nothing about it) that the good fairy had arranged for the Princess to have sweet dreams during her long slumber. Finally, after talking for four hours, they had yet to say half the things they wanted to say to one another.

The whole palace, however, had been awakened with the Princess. Everyone else was occupied with getting on with their duties, and since they were not all in love, they were ready to die of hunger. The lady-in-waiting, who was suffering as much as the rest, finally lost patience and in a loud voice called out to the Princess that supper was served.

The Prince helped the Princess to rise. She was already dressed, and splendidly, though the Prince was careful not to mention that, with her high collar, she was dressed a little like his grandmother—not that she was any less beautiful for it.

They passed into a salon hung with mirrors and dined there, served by the household stewards, while musicians played some ancient pieces of music on violins and oboes—and played them very well, considering they had not played them for a hundred years. When supper was over, without wasting a moment, they were married by the chaplain in the palace chapel, and retired to the Princess's golden bedroom, attended by the lady-in-waiting, who drew the curtains. They slept hardly at all. The Princess had little need of sleep, of course, and the Prince left as soon as morning came.

The Prince returned to the city to tell his father, who was anxiously awaiting his return, that he had become lost while hunting in the forest, but that he had passed the night in the hut of a charcoal-burner who had fed him black bread and cheese. His father, the king, a good-natured man, believed his son. But his mother found his story less persuasive. She knew the Prince went hunting nearly every day, and he always had some handy excuse when he stayed two or three nights away from home.

She felt certain that he was carrying on some amorous affair.

He lived with the Princess for more than two whole years, during which time they had two children. The first, a daughter, was called *Dawn*, while the second, a boy, was named *Day*, because he appeared even more beautiful than his sister.

The queen said many times to her son, in an attempt to get him to confide in her, that he must be quite content in his life, but he never dared trust her with his secret. Because even though he loved her, he feared her more, for she came from a race of ogres, and the king had only married her for her great wealth. Many whispered at court that she had an ogress's inclinations, and that when little children passed nearby, it was all she could do to stop herself from pouncing on them.

Small wonder then that the Prince was reluctant to say a word.

But after two years, when the king died and the Prince found himself on the throne, he declared publicly his marriage to the Princess, and went in great ceremony to fetch his Princess, now his Queen, from her palace. Alongside her two children, she made a magnificent entrance into the capital city.

Soon after the King went to war with his neighbor, the Emperor Cantalabutte. In his absence, he made the Queen Mother his regent, to rule the kingdom in his place, and entrusted his wife and children to her care. He expected to be at war all summer, and as soon as he was gone the Queen Mother sent her daughter-in-law and two grandchildren to a country mansion in the woods, so that she could more easily gratify her horrible appetite. She went to join them a few days later, and in the evening summoned the chief steward.

"For my dinner tomorrow," she told him, "I want to eat little Dawn."

"Oh, madam!" exclaimed the steward.

"That is what I want," said the Queen Mother (who spoke in the tones of an ogress who longs for fresh meat). "You will serve her with a Sauce Robert," she added.

This poor man, seeing plainly that it was pointless to toy with an ogress, took his carving knife and climbed up the stairs to the room of little Dawn. She was four years old, and when she came running to greet him, laughing and throwing her arms round his neck and asking for some sweets, he burst into tears and let the knife fall from his hands.

So he went down to the yard behind the house and slaughtered a little lamb. For this he made so delicious a sauce that his mistress declared she had never eaten anything so good. At the same time the steward carried little Dawn to his wife, and asked her to hide her in their quarters beside the barnyard.

Eight days later the wicked Queen Mother summoned her steward again.

"For my supper," she said, "I will eat little Day."

The steward made no protest, determined to fool her as he had done the time before. He went to fetch little Day, whom he found holding a small fencing sword, dueling with a big ape, even though he was only three years old. He carried him off to his wife, who hid him away with little Dawn. In place of Day, the steward served up to the ogress a young kid so tender that she found it irresistibly delicious.

Things had gone according to plan so far, but one evening the evil Queen Mother said to the steward, "I have a mind to eat the Queen with the same sauce you served with her children."

At this point the poor steward despaired of being able to deceive her again. The young Queen was twenty years old (not counting the hundred years she had slept), and her skin, though fair and beautiful, had become a little tough, and what animal in their barn could possibly pass for her? He concluded that, to save his own life, he must kill the Queen. He went upstairs to her room determined to commit the terrible deed once and for all. Working himself into a fury, he entered the young Queen's chamber with dagger in hand. Unwilling to take her by surprise, but with great deference, he told her of the command the Queen Mother had given him.

"Do your duty," she said, baring her neck to him. "Carry out the order given to you. Then I shall see my children once more, my poor children whom I loved so much!" No one had told her what had happened to her children when they were whisked away, and she believed them to be dead.

"No, no, madam," the poor steward replied, overcome with emotion. "You will not die, but you will see your children again. They are in my quarters, where I've hidden them. I will fool the Queen Mother again by serving her a young doe in your place."

With that he led her to his rooms and left her there to embrace and weep with her children. He then proceeded to prepare a doe so artfully that the Queen Mother ate it for her supper with as much relish as if it had been the young Queen.

The Queen Mother was quite pleased with herself and her cruelty, and planned to tell the King on his return that marauding wolves had devoured the Queen and their children. One evening, as was her habit, she was prowling about the courtyards and barnyards of the mansion in hope of scenting fresh meat and heard the little boy Day crying in a filthy cellar. The child was weeping because his mother had threatened to whip him for being mean—and then she heard the voice of Dawn begging forgiveness for her brother.

The ogress recognized the voices of the Queen and her children, and was furious to discover she had been deceived. The next morning, in tones so dreadful that everyone trembled, she ordered a huge vat to be brought into the middle of the courtyard. This she filled with all kinds of toads, vipers, snakes, and serpents, planning to cast into it the Queen and her children, the steward, his wife, and serving-girl. By her command they were brought forward with their hands tied behind their backs.

There they stood, with the Queen Mother's executioners preparing to cast them into the vat, when into the courtyard rode the King! Nobody had expected him back so soon, but he had traveled in great haste. Astonished, he demanded to know the meaning of the horrible spectacle that greeted him. No one dared tell him, when at that moment the ogress, enraged by what confronted her, threw herself head-first into the vat and was devoured instantly by the hideous creatures with which she had filled it.

The King could not help being sorry, for she was after all his mother, but he soon found consolation with his beautiful wife and children.

THE MORAL.

Waiting some time for a groom—
Gallant, sweet, rich, and handsome—
Never caused a bride any gloom,
But after a century spent sleepfully,
You won't find any woman
Who waited more peacefully.
The story still seems to want to make clear,
That by Cupid such matches are made,
That long delay should bring no less cheer,
Nothing is lost in the wait,
And love with such passion,
Inspires matrimonial faith—
Though I've not the courage to preach,
A moral that is so far out of reach.

Cinderella could not guess how a pumpkin
was going to get her to the Ball.

Cinderella

or, The Little Glass Slipper

NCE upon a time there was a kind, agreeable widower who took for his second wife the haughtiest, proudest woman who ever lived. She had two daughters, who possessed their mother's temper and resembled her in everything. The man, on the other hand, had a young daughter whose sweetness and kindness were without equal. These traits she got from her mother, who was the nicest woman who ever lived.

The nuptials were hardly over before the stepmother began to display her bad humor. She could not suffer this young girl's goodness, which made her own daughters seem that much more hateful by comparison. She ordered her to do all the most odious chores around the house—it was the girl who washed the dishes, cleaned the stairs, and swept out the rooms of her stepmother and her stepsisters. She slept on a nasty straw mattress in a dingy attic at the top of the house, while the sisters had rooms with parquet floors, stylish and comfortable beds, and full-length mirrors in which they could admire themselves.

The poor girl endured it all with patience and dared not complain to her father, who would only have scolded her, because he was ruled entirely by his wife. When she had finished her work, she would go to a corner of the fireplace and sit among the ashes and cinders, and it was from this that she came to be called *Cinder-butt*. It was the younger stepsister—who was not quite as spiteful or crude as the elder—who dubbed her *Cinderella*. However, even in her wretched rags, Cinderella remained a hundred times more beautiful than her stepsisters, for all their splendid clothes.

Now it so happened that one day the king's son announced he was throwing a Ball, and he invited everyone of quality. The two young ladies were also invited, for they were prominent figures in the country. So they were quite pleased and were soon busy choosing the clothes and hairstyles that suited them best. All this just meant more drudgery for Cinderella, for it was she who ironed her stepsisters' linens and sewed their ruffles. They could talk of nothing else but the latest styles.

"For myself," said the elder, "I will wear my red velvet dress with the English lace."

"I have only my everyday petticoat," said the younger, "but to make up for it I shall wear my cloak with the golden flowers and my bodice of diamonds, which are not so bad."

They sent for the best stylist to arrange their head-dresses and pin up their hair, and bought beauty marks from the most fashionable maker.

They summoned Cinderella to get her opinion, for she had good taste. Cinderella gave them the best possible advice, and even offered to comb their hair, to which they gladly agreed.

As she was grooming them, they said to her, "Cinderella, wouldn't you like to go to the Ball?"

"Alas, my sisters," said Cinderella, "you're making fun of me. That would be no place for me."

"That is so true," they said. "People would have a good laugh to see a Cinder-butt at the Ball."

Anyone but Cinderella would have tangled their hair in knots, but she was too good-natured and finished their hair to perfection. Her stepsisters were so transported with joy that they went nearly two days without eating. They broke more than a dozen laces by tightening them too tight so as to make their waists more slender, and they were forever in front of their mirror.

At last the happy day arrived. Away they went, Cinderella following them with her eyes as far as she could. When they were out of sight, she began to cry.

Her Godmother found her in tears and asked her what was the matter.

She stammered, "I would like…I would like…" But she was crying so hard that she could not finish.

Her Godmother, who was a Fairy Godmother, said, "You would like to go to the Ball, wouldn't you?"

"Oh, yes," said Cinderella with a sigh.

"Well, if you will be a good girl," her Godmother said, "I will get you there." She led Cinderella into her room and said, "Go into the garden and bring me a pumpkin."

Cinderella went at once and picked the finest one she could find and carried it in to her Godmother, though she could not guess how a pumpkin was going to get her to the Ball.

Her Godmother scooped out the pumpkin, and when only the outer flesh was left, struck it with her wand. Instantly, the pumpkin was transformed into a beautiful golden coach.

Then her Godmother went and looked in the mousetrap, where she found six mice still alive. She told Cinderella to lift the door of the mousetrap a little, and as each one came out she gave it a tap with her wand that changed each mouse into a beautiful horse, until there was a fine team of six dappled, mouse-gray horses.

But the Fairy Godmother worried about how to provide a coachman.

"I will go and see," said Cinderella, "if there is a rat in the rat trap. We could make a coachman of him."

"Quite right," said her Godmother, "go and see."

Cinderella brought in the rat trap, which contained three big rats. The Fairy chose one on account of his elegant whiskers, and as soon as she touched him, he turned into a fat coachman with the most magnificent mustache you've ever seen.

"Now go into the garden," her Godmother said, "and bring me the six lizards that you will find behind the watering can."

No sooner had Cinderella fetched them than her Godmother turned them into six footmen, who immediately climbed on the back of the coach in their richly colored liveries, and hung on there as if they had never done anything else in all their lives.

Then the Fairy Godmother said, "Well, there you have the means of going to the Ball. Will that do?"

"Um, yes," she said, "but must I go like this, in my ragged clothes?"

Her Godmother merely touched her with her wand, and instantly her clothes were changed into a gown of gold and silver cloth, encrusted with colorful jewels. Then her Godmother gave her a pair of glass slippers, the prettiest in the world.

Thus transformed, she stepped into the coach. Her Godmother strongly advised her not to stay at the Ball past midnight, warning her that if she did, her coach would turn back into a pumpkin, her horses and footmen would once again become mice and lizards, and her clothes would resume their former ragged state.

Cinderella promised her Godmother that she would not fail to leave the Ball before midnight, and away she went, beside herself with joy.

The Prince, told of the arrival of a great princess no one had ever heard of, hurried out to receive her. He gave her his hand to help her down from the coach and led her into the hall where the company was assembled. All at once a great silence fell over the room. Dancers stopped dancing, musicians stopped playing, people stopped talking—so rapt was the attention directed to this beautiful stranger. The only sounds were confused whispers of "Who is that?" and "Oh, how lovely she is!" Even the king, old as he was, could not take his eyes off her and whispered to the queen that it had been a long time since he had seen anyone as beautiful and charming. All the ladies craned their necks to examine her hair and her clothes, determined to copy them the next day, assuming they could find fabrics as fine, and tailors as accomplished.

The Prince seated her in the place of honor and then asked her to dance. She danced with such grace that admiration for her only grew. A wonderful banquet was served, but the young Prince could eat nothing,

The only sounds were confused whispers of "Who is that?"
and "Oh, how lovely she is!"

so preoccupied was he with watching her. She went
and sat beside her stepsisters and paid them a thousand compliments, and shared with them the oranges
and lemons that the king had given her—all of which
greatly astonished them, for they did not recognize her.

While they were chatting, Cinderella heard the clock
strike a quarter to midnight. She made a deep curtsy

to the other guests and then made her way out of the hall as quickly as she could. As soon as she got home, she found her Godmother to thank her. She said that she wished to go once more to the Ball the next day, because the Prince had invited her. While she was busy telling her Godmother everything that had happened, her two stepsisters knocked at the door. Cinderella let them in.

"What a long time you've been away," she said with a yawn, rubbing her eyes and stretching out as if she had only just woken up. In truth, she hadn't had a thought of sleeping for even a moment since they'd left.

"If you had been at the Ball," said one of her step-sisters, "you would not be weary. There came a most beautiful princess, the most beautiful that has ever been seen, and she praised us a thousand times and gave us her oranges and lemons."

Cinderella could hardly express the joy she felt. She asked them the name of the princess, but they admitted that no one knew her, and that the Prince's heart ached so that he would give anything to know who she was.

Cinderella smiled, and remarked that she must have been beautiful indeed. "How lucky you are," she said. "Couldn't I go and see her? Oh, please, Javotte, lend me the yellow dress that you wear every day."

"Really!" said Javotte. "To think I would lend my dress to a grubby Cinder-butt like you—I'd have to be out of my mind."

Cinderella had expected this refusal, was in fact glad of it, for she would have been in a tricky spot had her sister actually been willing to lend her a dress.

The next day the two sisters went to the Ball, and so did Cinderella, even more splendidly dressed than the first time. The Prince stayed glued to her side, whispering sweet nothings in her ear the whole time. She enjoyed herself so much and was so distracted that she forgot her Godmother's warning, and when the first stroke of midnight fell upon her ears, she at first thought it was not yet past eleven. She shot up and fled the Ball as nimbly as a deer. The Prince followed but could not catch her. As she was running away, however, one of her glass slippers fell off her foot, and this the Prince picked up with tender care.

When Cinderella reached home she was out of breath, without her coach, her footmen, or her horses, and back in her ragged clothes. Nothing remained of her splendid outfit except for one of the little glass slippers, the mate of the one that fell off her other foot.

The palace guards were asked if they had not seen a princess leave through the gate, but they swore they had seen no one, other than a girl dressed in rags who looked more like a peasant woman than a young lady.

When her stepsisters returned from the Ball, Cinderella asked them if they had enjoyed themselves once again, and if the beautiful lady had been there.

They said yes, but that the lady had fled when the bells tolled midnight, and in such haste that she lost one of her little glass slippers. The Prince had picked it up and then done nothing but gaze at it for the rest of the Ball—he was no doubt very much in love with the slipper's beautiful owner.

They spoke the truth, for a few days later, the Prince trumpeted the news all over the kingdom that he would marry the one whose foot fit the glass slipper.

They tried it first on the princesses, then on the duchesses and the whole court, but all in vain. They brought it to the home of Cinderella's stepsisters, who did everything they could to squeeze one of their feet into the slipper. But in the end it was no use.

Cinderella, who was looking on and recognized her slipper, laughed and said, "Let's see if it would be a good fit for me."

Her sisters burst out laughing and began to mock her, but the gentleman who was trying on the slipper looked closely at Cinderella. Finding her very beautiful, he said that it seemed only fair, and that his orders were to try the slipper on every maiden. He had Cinderella sit down and, putting the slipper on her little foot, saw that it slid on with no difficulty and was molded to the shape of her foot like wax.

To say her stepsisters were surprised at this turn of events would be an understatement. But it was nothing

*Putting the slipper on her little foot, he saw that it slid on
with no difficulty and was molded to the shape of her foot like wax.*

compared to their astonishment when Cinderella drew from her pocket the other glass slipper, which she then slid on her other foot.

At this moment, her Fairy Godmother appeared and tapped her wand on Cinderella's clothes, transforming them into even an more magnificent ensemble than the ones before.

Then her two stepsisters recognized her for the beautiful lady they had seen at the Ball. They threw themselves at her feet, begging forgiveness for all the ill-treatment she had suffered at their hands. Cinderella picked them up, and said as she embraced them that she pardoned them with all her heart and begged them to love her always.

She was taken to the palace of the young Prince in her new dress. He found her more beautiful than ever, and they were married a few days later. Cinderella was as good as she was beautiful. She arranged lodging in the palace for her two stepsisters and married them the very same day to two great lords of the court.

THE MORAL.

Beauty's a rare treasure for the fairer sex,
Admiration of it will never end, I expect.
But what of good grace, and all that it will?
There's a gift without price and rarer still.

Cinderella from her Godmother Fairy,
Received this gift, it would seem,
So much so that she became Queen:
(Such a moral of the tale is necessary.)

Next to this gift, beauty is quite ordinary,
For grace is the true gift of the Fairies—
It won the Prince's heart at the fancy-dress Ball.
Without it one can do naught, with it one can do all.

ANOTHER.

No doubt, it's a great advantage,
To possess spirit and courage,
Good birth and common sense,
And many other like talents,
Parceled out and received from Heaven;
But you may take them or leave them,
For your advancement, or any other's,
If you ignore the advice of Godmothers.

"Help, help! the Marquis of Carabas is drowning!"

Puss in Boots

HERE once was a miller who died and left his three sons all his worldly possessions— his mill, his donkey, and his cat. These were quickly divided among them, without consulting the notary or the local attorney, who would have soon gobbled up all the proceeds of the humble inheritance.

The eldest son took the mill, the second son took the donkey, and the youngest son was left with the cat. He was more than a little disappointed at getting the leftover crumbs from his father's estate. "My brothers," he lamented, "will be able to make a decent living by combining forces, but as for me, once I have eaten the cat and made a muff out of his hide, I'm bound to die of hunger."

These last words were overheard by Puss, who pretended not to have been listening, and said to him with a calm and serious air, "Do not worry, master. All you need do is give me a pouch and make me a pair of boots for going into in the woods. You will see that you did not inherit such a poor share as you think."

As the cat had shown himself capable of performing quite a few nifty tricks—catching rats and mice by hanging upside-down by his feet or hiding in the grain and playing dead—his master was not entirely without hope that Puss could somehow rescue him from his miserable plight.

So when Puss got what he'd asked for, he pulled his boots on cheerfully and hung the pouch around his neck, holding the cords that tied it with his paws. He went off to a warren where he knew there were many rabbits, placed some lettuce and bran in his pouch, stretched out on the ground as if her were dead, and waited for some young rabbit, naïve in the ways of the world, to come along and stuff himself in the pouch to get at the food he had put there.

No sooner had he lay down than his plans were realized. A gullible young rabbit crawled into the pouch, Puss pulled the cords tight, and killed him just like that. Very pleased with his capture, Puss marched off to the palace of the King and asked to speak with him. He was ushered up to His Majesty's apartment and bowed reverently to the King.

"I bring you, Sire," said Puss, "a rabbit from the warren of the Marquis of Carabas (the title he invented for his master), which he instructed me to present to you on his behalf."

"Tell your master," replied the King, "that I thank him, and that his gift pleases me."

Another time the cat hid himself in a wheat field, keeping the mouth of his pouch wide open. Two partridges ventured in, and by pulling the cords tight he captured them both. Off he went and presented them to the King, as he had done with the rabbit. His Majesty was no less pleased by the partridges and invited Puss to have a drink with him.

For two or three months, Puss continued on this way, from time to time taking some game he had caught to the King as a present from his master. One day, when he learned that the King was going to take his daughter, the most beautiful Princess, for a walk along the riverbank, he said to his master, "If you do as I tell you, your fortune is made. You just have to go and bathe in the river where I show you, and I'll do the rest."

The "Marquis of Carabas" had no idea what good it could possibly do, but he did what the cat told him. While he was bathing in the river, the King's carriage approached, and Puss at once began to cry out at the top of his voice, "Help, help! the Marquis of Carabas is drowning!"

At these shouts the King put his head out of the carriage window. He recognized the cat who had so often brought him game, and ordered his guards to rescue the Marquis of Carabas. While they were pulling the confused Marquis out of the river, Puss approached the carriage and explained to the King that, while his master was bathing, robbers had come and stolen his clothes, even though he had cried "Stop, thieves!" at the top of his lungs. (In fact, the crafty cat had hidden them under a big rock.) The King at once commanded the stewards of his wardrobe to go and retrieve a suit of his finest clothes for the Marquis of Carabas.

The King gave the Marquis a thousand compliments, as the fine clothes he had just donned only heightened his good looks (for he was already handsome, if not usually so well-dressed). The King's daughter found him very much to her liking. Indeed, the Marquis of Carabas had not given her more than two or three tender, but respectful glances before she fell madly in love with him. The King invited him to climb into the coach and join their party.

Delighted to see that his plan was beginning to succeed, Puss went on ahead of them and soon came upon some peasants who were mowing a pasture.

"Listen, my good people," he said, "if you do not tell the King that the meadow you are mowing belongs to the Marquis of Carabas, you will all be hacked up into small pieces like chopped liver."

*"If you do not, you will all be hacked up into small pieces
like chopped liver.*

When the King came along and asked the mowers to
whom the pasture belonged, they promptly replied, "To the
Marquis of Carabas," for the cat's threat had duly scared
them.

"You have a fine inheritance there," the King said to the
Marquis of Carabas.

"You see, Sire," replied the Marquis, "it's a meadow that never fails to yield an abundant crop every year."

Still traveling ahead, Puss came upon some harvesters. "Listen, my good people," he said, "if you do not swear that all of these fields of wheat belong to the Marquis of Carabas, you will all be hacked up into small pieces like chopped liver."

When the King came by a moment later and wished to know who owned the wheat fields, the harvesters all replied, "To the Marquis of Carabas."

And the King was even more pleased with the Marquis.

The cat, who continued to go ahead of the coach, made the same threat to everyone he met, and the King grew astounded at the vast possessions of the Marquis of Carabas.

Finally, Puss arrived at a magnificent castle, the lord of which was an Ogre. He was the richest Ogre anyone had ever seen, for all the lands through which the King had just passed were part of his domain. The cat had been careful to find out who this Ogre was and what he could do. He asked to speak with him, insisting that he could never pass so close to this castle without paying his respects to its owner.

The Ogre received the cat as civilly as an ogre can, and asked him to sit down.

*The cat had been careful to find out who this Ogre was
and what he could do.*

The Ogre received the cat as civilly as an ogre can.

"I have been told," Puss said to him, "that you have the ability to transform yourself into any kind of beast—that you could, for example, change yourself into a lion or an elephant."

"It is true," the Ogre said brusquely, "and to prove it, watch me as I become a lion."

Puss was so frightened on seeing a lion suddenly appear before him that he sprang onto the roof—not without some difficulty and danger, mind you, for his boots were not made for walking on tiles. Upon seeing that the Ogre had changed back, Puss climbed back down and admitted to having been terrified.

"I have also been told," he added, "though I could hardly believe it, that you also have the ability to take the form of the smallest animals—for example, that you could change yourself into a rat or even a mouse—which, I have to say, I find to be quite impossible."

"Impossible?" cried the Ogre. "Watch me!" And at that moment the Ogre changed himself into a mouse and began to scurry about the floor. No sooner did Puss see that than he pounced on the little mouse and ate it.

Meanwhile the King was passing by, and noticing the Ogre's beautiful castle, he desired to go inside. Puss, who heard the rumble of the carriage as it crossed the drawbridge, dashed out to the courtyard and hailed the King, "Welcome, Your Majesty, to the castle of the Marquis of Carabas!"

"Why, Marquis!" cried the King. "You mean to say this castle belongs to you as well? Nothing could be finer than this courtyard and the surrounding buildings. Let's see what they look like inside, if you please."

The Marquis gave his hand to the young Princess and followed the King, who led them inside. Entering a great hall, they found a magnificent spread the Ogre had laid out for his friends, whom he had planned to entertain that day. But his friends dared not enter when they found out that the King was there.

The King was now as charmed by the excellent qualities of the Marquis of Carabas as his daughter, who was over the moon for him. Noting the great wealth the Marquis obviously possessed, and after five or six cups of wine, he turned to the Marquis and said, "It is up to you, Marquis, whether or not you will be my son-in-law."

The Marquis, bowing very deeply, accepted the honor that the King offered him, and on the same day he married the Princess.

Puss, for his part, became a great lord and gave up the hunting of mice—except for amusement.

THE ORAL.

However great an advantage,
Gained by a wealthy heritage,
Passed down from father to son,
When it comes to the young,
Industry, know-how, and wit
Prove far superior to it.

NOTHER.

If a miller's son, with such quickness,
Can win the heart of a Princess,
Who eyes him with passionate fire,
His means of inflaming desire—
His dress, his good looks, and his youth—
Are more than indifferent, in truth.

Riquet with the Tuft

NCE upon a time there was a Queen who bore a son so ugly and misshapen that for a long time many doubted that he was human. But a Fairy who was present at his birth promised the Queen that he would not go without love, for he would have a brilliant mind. And, she added, that by virtue of the gift she had just given him, he would be able to give the person he loved as much intelligence as he possessed.

This consoled the poor Queen a little, but she was still greatly distressed at having brought such a little monster into the world. However, hardly had the child learned to talk than he was speaking in a most articulate way, and had a witty demeanor about him that everyone was charmed by.

Oh, I forgot to mention—on the day he was born he had a little tuft of hair on his head. And so he was called "Riquet with the Tuft," as Riquet was his family name.

Seven or eight years later, the queen of a neighboring kingdom gave birth to twin daughters. The first one to come into the world was more beautiful than the dawn, and the queen was so pleased, it was feared her great joy might actually cause her harm. The same Fairy who had assisted at the birth of Riquet with the Tuft was there, and in order to temper the the queen's excitement, she declared that this little Princess would have no sense at all and would be as stupid as she was beautiful.

This greatly mortified the queen, and a moment or two later her sorrow was increased, for the second daughter proved to be extremely ugly.

"Do not grieve, madam," said the Fairy, "your daughter shall be compensated in another way. She will have so much good sense that her lack of beauty will scarcely be noticed."

"May Heaven grant it!" said the queen. "But is there no means by which the elder, who is so beautiful, can be endowed with some intelligence?"

"As far as wits, madam, I can do nothing for her," replied the Fairy. "But with regard to beauty, I can do anything. As there is nothing I would not do to please you, I will bestow upon her the power of making handsome or beautiful the person who pleases her most."

As the two princesses grew, their perfections grew with them, and it seemed no one could talk of anything but the beauty of the elder and the wit of the younger. But it was likewise true that their defects also increased as they grew older. The younger girl only got uglier. And the older girl became stupider with each passing day. Either she failed to respond when asked a question or replied with something inane. At the same time she was so awkward that she could not set four china vases on the mantelpiece without smashing one of them, nor drink a glass of water without spilling half of it over her clothes.

Although beauty is a great advantage for a young person, the ugly princess almost always surpassed the pretty one in any gathering. At first they fawned in admiration over the older Princess's beauty, but soon after they were drawn to the younger's wit and wisdom, enthralled by the thoughts she shared and the way she shared them. In a matter of minutes, the older Princess was left all by herself while everyone crowded around the younger.

The elder Princess was not so stupid that she did not notice this, and she would gladly have given all her beauty for half her sister's cleverness. Her mother the queen, as wise as she was, could not help but reproach her from time to time for her lack of sense, the thought of which made the poor girl want to die of grief.

One day the Princess had withdrawn to a wood to lament her misfortune, when she saw a little man approach, terribly ugly and unpleasant but splendidly dressed. It was the young prince, Riquet with the Tuft. He had fallen in love with her portrait, which had been dispersed widely, and had left his father's kingdom in order to have the pleasure of seeing and talking to her. Delighted to encounter her alone, he approached with the utmost respect and courtesy. But after paying her the customary compliments, he noticed how melancholy she seemed.

"I do not understand, madam," he said, "how a person as beautiful as you are can be as sad as you appear. Though I can boast of having seen countless beautiful ladies, I can honestly say that never have I seen one whose beauty compares to yours."

"It is kind of you to say so, sir," replied the Princess, and stopped there, not knowing what else to say.

"Beauty," said Riquet, "is such a great advantage that it must override all else, and when you have it, I cannot imagine anything that could cause you much grief."

"I would much prefer," said the Princess, "to be as ugly as you and have sense than be as beautiful as I am and as stupid."

"Nothing more clearly displays good sense, madam, than to believe you do not possess it. And thus the more sense you have, the more you fear it to be lacking."

"I'm not so sure about that," said the Princess. "But I do know that I am very stupid, and this is the reason for the misery that plagues me."

"If that is all that troubles you, madam, I can easily put an end to your pain."

"And how will you do that?" asked the Princess.

"I have the power, madam," said Riquet with the Tuft, "to bestow as much good sense as it is possible to possess on the person I love the most—and you are that person. So it is up to you if you would have so much intelligence, provided your are willing to marry me."

The Princess was dumbstruck and said nothing.

"I can see," Riquet continued, "that this proposition troubles you, and I am not surprised. But I will give you a whole year to make up your mind."

The Princess had so little sense, and at the same time desired it so fervently, that she deluded herself that the end of this year would never come. So she accepted the offer he made to her. No sooner had she given her word to Riquet that she would marry him within one year than she felt a complete change come over her. She found she could say all that she wanted to say with ease, and to say it in an erudite, finished, and natural manner. She engaged Riquet in a deep and lengthy conversation, holding her own so well that Riquet worried he had given her more intelligence than he had himself.

When she returned to the palace, the entire court was struck by the sudden and extraordinary change in her. As much as they had become used to hearing her say silly, impertinent things, now they only heard her say things that were sensible and infinitely wise. The whole court was overjoyed—with the exception of her younger sister, for as she no longer had the advantage over the elder in intelligence, she now seemed like nothing but a blundering ape in comparison.

The king himself began to seek his elder daughter's advice, and sometimes held his council in her apartment. Murmurs of this change having spread abroad, princes of the neighboring kingdoms made efforts to endear themselves to her. Almost all asked for her hand in marriage. But she found none had enough wit, and so she listened to every one without committing to any.

However, one did come at last who was so powerful, so rich, so witty, and so handsome that she could not help being inclined to him. Her father, having noticed this, told her she could make her own choice of husband, that she had only to declare herself.

Now the more sense you have, the more difficult it is to make up your mind in an affair of this kind. After thanking her father, she asked that he give her time to think it over. In order to ponder over her decision without distraction, she went for a walk in a wood—the very wood, as it happened, where she had met Riquet with the Tuft. While she walked, deep in thought, she heard a thudding underfoot, as though many people were running busily back and forth. Bending an ear toward the ground, she heard voices. "Bring me that pot," said one, "Give me this boiler," said another, and then, "Put some wood on the fire!"

At this point the earth opened beneath her feet, and she saw below what appeared to be a large kitchen full of cooks and scullions, and all the attendants that the preparation of a great banquet requires. A gang of some twenty or thirty rotisserie-turners emerged and took up their positions around a long table in a path in the wood. They all, with their basters in hand and their chef's caps on one side of their head, worked in rhythm to the sound of a harmonious song.

The Princess, astonished by this spectacle, asked them for whom they were doing all this work.

"For Prince Riquet with the Tuft, madam," said the leader of the crew. "His wedding is tomorrow."

Now the Princess was even more shocked than before, remembering suddenly that it had been a year to the day since she had promised to marry Prince Riquet with the Tuft. She felt like she'd just fallen from a great height. When she'd made the promise, she had still been stupid, and when the Prince had given her reason, she'd forgot all her nonsense, including her promise.

The earth opened beneath her feet, and she saw below what appeared to be a large kitchen full of cooks and scullions.

She had not taken another thirty steps before Riquet with the Tuft appeared in front of her, gallant and magnificent, just like a prince on the eve of his wedding day.

"You see, madam," he said, "I have kept my word, and I have no doubt that you have come to keep yours and, by giving me your hand, make me the happiest man alive."

"I should be frank with you," replied the Princess. "I have not yet made up my mind about that, and I'm not sure I'll ever be able to make the decision you wish."

"You surprise me, madam," said Riquet with the Tuft.

"I don't doubt it," said the Princess, "and surely, if I were dealing with an unfeeling brute or a man without sense, I would feel very embarrassed. 'A princess must keep her word,' he would say, 'and you must marry me because you promised to!' But I am speaking to a most intelligent man, and I am sure that he will listen to reason. You know that even when I had no sense I could not make up my mind to marry you. How do you expect me now, having gained the intelligence you gave me (which only makes me harder to please), to make a decision I couldn't make then? If you really wanted me to marry you, you should not have relieved me of my stupidity and enabled me to see more clearly than I did."

"If a man without sense," said Riquet with the Tuft, "would be expected, as you have just said, to reproach you for breaking your word, why do you expect me, madam, to act differently over a thing that may determine the happiness of my entire life? Is it reasonable that people who have sense should be treated worse than those who have none? Would you claim that for yourself—you, who so decidedly have sense, and desired so ardently to have it? But let's get down to the facts, please. Except for my ugliness, is there anything about me that you dislike? Are you dissatisfied with my breeding, my brains, my temperament, or my manners?"

"Not at all," replied the Princess. "I love in you all of the qualities you speak of."

"If that is so," said Riquet with the Tuft, "I shall be happy since you have it in your power to make me the most charming of all men."

"How can that be so?" asked the Princess.

"It will be so," replied Riquet with the Tuft, "if you love me enough to wish it to be so. And so that you do not doubt me, madam, know that the same Fairy who on the day of my birth gave me the power of bestowing intelligence upon the person I loved, likewise gave you the power to bestow beauty on the person you would love and would wish to confer this favor."

"If that is so," said the Princess, "I wish with all my heart that you may become the most beautiful and charming prince in the world, and I make a gift of it to you as much as it is to me."

No sooner had the Princess uttered these words than Riquet with the Tuft appeared before her eyes as the most graceful, handsome, and charming man that she had ever seen.

Some claim that this was not the enchantment of a fairy at work, but that love alone brought about the metamorphosis. They say that the Princess, as she mused upon her lover's perseverance and his discretion, and the many admirable qualities of his head and his heart, no longer saw the deformity of his body nor the ugliness of his face. His hunch seemed no more than was natural in a man with a broad back, and what she had previously considered a frightful limp, she now saw merely as a charming eccentricity. They also say that she found his eyes, which were darkly shaded, shone that much brighter for her, and that this defect was to her but a mark of excessive passion, while his big red nose was martial and heroic.

Whatever the case, the Princess promised to marry him at once, provided only that he obtained the consent of her father the king. The king knew Riquet with the

Tuft to be a prince both witty and wise, and on learn-
ing of his daughter's affection for him, he accepted
him with pleasure as his son-in-law. The wedding took
place the next day, just as Riquet with the Tuft had
foreseen, and according to the arrangements he had
made long in advance.

THE ORAL.

In this fairy tale what we find,
Is more plain truth than otherwise:
All we love is beauty to our eyes,
All we love has a beautiful mind.

ANOTHER.

All the gifts of beauty in nature,
Are less able to make a heart tender,
Than a single invisible pleasure,
That love, in its mystery, can render.

Donkey-Skin

NCE upon a time there was a King so great, so loved by his people, and so respected by all his neighbors and allies that it could be said that he was the happiest monarch alive. His happiness had only been enhanced by the choice he had made for a wife—a princess as beautiful as she was virtuous. This happy couple lived in perfect harmony. From their faithful union was born a girl endowed with so much grace and so many charms that they never regretted having only one child.

Magnificence, good taste, and abundance reigned in the King's palace. The ministers were wise and skillful, the courtiers virtuous and devoted, and the servants faithful and industrious. The vast stables were filled with the most beautiful horses in the world, covered with rich caparisons. But what most surprised strangers who came to admire these stables was that, in the most prominent stall, stood a marvelous donkey with great long ears. It was not out of whimsy but with good reason that the King had given this donkey a special and distinguished place. The virtues of this rare animal deserved distinction, since nature had made him in so extraordinary a way that his litter, instead of being fouled, was covered every morning with an abundance of beautiful gold coins—*écus au soleil* and *Louis d'ors* of every kind—which the grooms collected each day when he woke.

Now, as the vicissitudes of life befall Kings as much as their subjects, and goods are always mixed with a few evils, fate decreed that the Queen be taken by a terrible illness, against which, despite science and the skill of the doctors, no cure could be found. The kingdom was in mourning.

The King, tender-hearted and still very much in love—despite the famous proverb that "marriage is the tomb of love"—was despondent in his grief and made fervent vows to all the temples in his kingdom, and offered to give his life for that of his dear wife. But the gods and the fairies were invoked in vain.

The Queen, feeling her last hour approach, called for her husband, now dissolved into tears, and said, "Allow me, before I die, to ask one thing of you. It is this: if you wish to remarry…"

At these words the King broke into pitiful cries, took his wife's hands, baptized with his tears, and assured her that it was useless to speak to him of a second marriage. "No, my dear Queen," he said at last, "speak to me rather of how I may follow you."

"The state," replied the Queen with a strength that only increased the King's grief, "the state demands successors, and since I have only given you a daughter, I must urge you to have sons who take after you. But I ask you, by all the love you have had for me, not to yield to the zeal of your people until you have found a princess more beautiful and more graceful than I. I want your oath, and then I shall die happy."

Presumably, the Queen, who was not lacking in self-esteem, had demanded this oath believing there was no other in the world whose beauty could match hers, and thus make sure that the King would never remarry.

Finally, she died. Never did a husband make such a mournful racket. Moaning and sobbing day and night—the meager privilege of being a widower—were his sole occupation.

Even great sorrows do not last, however. And it was only a matter of time before the great lords of the kingdom assembled and came before the King to petition him to remarry. This request seemed callous to him and caused him to shed fresh tears. He reminded them of the oath he had made to the Queen and defied his counselors to find a princess more beautiful and of better figure than her, thinking it would be impossible.

The great lords assembled and came before the King to petition him to remarry, which caused him to shed fresh tears.

But the council regarded such a promise as merely a trifle and said that beauty didn't count for much as long as the queen was virtuous and fertile. For the state needed princes for its peace and prosperity, even though, in truth, the King's daughter had all the qualities required to make a great queen. But a foreign prince would have to be chosen for her husband, and then this stranger would take her back to his home.

And even if, instead, he remained in the land and reigned alongside her, their children would not be considered to be of the same bloodline as the King, and so, there being no prince of his name, neighboring peoples would stir up wars, which would bring about the ruin of the kingdom.

The King, impressed by these considerations, promised that he would try to satisfy them. And so he searched among the eligible princesses for one that would suit him. Every day they brought him charming portraits, but none had the grace of his late Queen, so he could not make up his mind.

Unfortunately, he noticed that his daughter, the Princess, was not only beautiful and had a ravishing figure, but that she even surpassed her mother, the Queen, in wit and charm. Her youth and the pleasant freshness of her glowing complexion inflamed the King with a desire so overpowering that he could not hide it from the Princess. He told her that he had resolved to marry *her*, since only she could release him from his oath.

The young Princess, full of virtue and modesty, nearly fainted at this horrifying proposition. She threw herself at the feet of her father the King and implored him, with all the strength of spirit she could muster, not to compel her to commit such a crime.

The King, who had set his mind upon this perverse notion, consulted an old Druid to put the young

The King, who had set his mind upon this perverse notion,
consulted an old Druid.

Princess's conscience at ease. This Druid, who was less spiritual than ambitious, sacrificed the cause of innocence and virtue to securing the favor of a great monarch, and so diminished the crime the King planned to commit that in the end he'd persuaded him that to marry his own daughter constituted a pious act.

The King, encouraged by the words of this scoundrel, embraced him and returned more stubbornly committed to this madness than ever. Thus he ordered the Princess to prepare to do as he wished.

The young Princess, outraged and in great distress, could think of no other recourse but the Lilac Fairy, her Godmother. To that end, she set out that same night in a small, two-wheeled carriage drawn by a large sheep who knew all the paths. Luckily, she got there.

When she did arrive, the Fairy, who loved the Princess, told her that she knew all she had come to say, but that she need not worry, for nothing could harm her if she faithfully followed the Fairy's instructions. "For, my dear child," she said to her, "it would be a great offense to marry your father, but you can avoid his command without contradicting it. Tell him that, to fulfill your fondest desire, he must give you a dress the color of the sky. Never, with all of his love and power, will he be able to achieve that."

The Princess thanked her Godmother with all her heart and the next morning told the King what the

The young Princess, outraged and in great distress, could think of no other recourse but the Lilac Fairy, her Godmother.

She set out that same night in a small, two-wheeled carriage
drawn by a large sheep who knew all the paths.

Fairy had advised her, insisting that no one could win her hand unless he gave her a dress the color of the sky.

The King, delighted with the hope this gave him, assembled the most skilled tailors and commanded them to create this dress, on the condition that if they did not, he would hang them all. He was saved from this drastic measure, however, for on the second day they brought him the much desired dress. The heavens, ringed with golden clouds, are not a more beautiful blue than that lovely dress was when it was laid out.

The Princess was desolate as a result and did not know what to do. The King pressed his case, and it was necessary for the Princess to once again resort to her Fairy Godmother. The Fairy, astonished that her plan had not succeeded, now told her to ask for another gown, this one the color of the Moon.

The King, who could not refuse her anything, again sent for the cleverest dressmakers and commanded them to make a dress the color of the Moon, and to deliver it within twenty-four hours, or else. The Princess, pleased by the superb dress they fashioned but not by the persistence of her father, cried bitterly once she was among her ladies-in-waiting and her nurse.

The Lilac Fairy, who knew about all that had happened, came to the aid of the poor Princess and said to her, "Unless I am very much mistaken, I believe that if you ask for a dress that is the color of the Sun, we will finally confound your father the King, because they will never be able to make such a dress—and if not, at least we buy some time."

So the Princess agreed and asked for the dress. The besotted King gladly contributed all the diamonds and rubies from his crown to help with this stellar project, commanding the tailors to spare nothing to make this dress as brilliant as the Sun. And, indeed, once the dress was unveiled, those who saw it were forced to close their eyes, it was so dazzling. (It is from this time that green spectacles and smoked crystal originate.)

How did the Princess respond to this sight? No one had ever seen anything so beautiful and artistically crafted. She was dumbstruck and, with the excuse that its brilliance hurt her eyes, retired to her chamber, where she found the Fairy waiting for her, more embarrassed than she could say.

Upon seeing the dress the color of the Sun, the Lilac Fairy turned red with anger. "Oh!" she said to the Princess, "this time we will put your father's unworthy love to a terrible test. He is being very stubborn about this marriage, which he believes is so close to happening, but I think he will be surprised by the request I advise you to make: tell him that he must give you the skin of that donkey he loves so dearly and that provides such a profusion of riches. Go, and make sure you tell him that you want that skin."

The Princess, happy to find another way out of a marriage she detested, and believing that her father could never bring himself to sacrifice his prize donkey, found him and made her latest demand: the hide of this noble animal.

Although the King was taken aback by this desire, he did not hesitate to satisfy it. The poor donkey was sacrificed and the skin brought with due ceremony to the Princess, who no longer saw any means of avoiding her misfortune and fell into despair.

As the Princess was tearing her hair and clutching her lovely cheeks, her Fairy Godmother came running and said to her, "What are you doing, my child? This is the happiest moment of your life. Wrap yourself in this skin, leave the palace, and walk for as long as the ground will carry you. When one sacrifices everything to virtue, the gods know how to reward it. Go, and I will take care that your possessions will follow. Wherever you stop, your chest with your clothes and your jewelry will be. And here is my wand, which I will give to you—tap the ground with it when you have need of the chest, and it will appear before your eyes. But make haste to leave, and do not delay."

The Princess kissed her Godmother a thousand times and begged her not to abandon her. Then, after smearing herself with chimney soot, donned that ugly skin and left the royal palace without being recognized by anyone.

The Princess's absence caused a great commotion. The King, who had prepared a magnificent feast, was inconsolable. He sent more than a hundred royal guards and more than a thousand musketeers to seek out his daughter. But the Fairy who protected her made her invisible to the most skillful searches, so there was no need to fear.

Meanwhile the Princess walked on. She went far, far, even farther, and looked everywhere for a place to rest. But, even though people gave her something to eat out of charity, she was so filthy that no one wanted to take her in. But after a time, she came to a beautiful city, at the gate of which was a farm where the farmer's wife had need of a wench to do the dishes and clean out the pens of the turkeys and pigs. Seeing such a dirty vagrant as the Princess appeared to be, she offered to take her in, which the Princess accepted gladly, so exhausted was she from walking.

She was put into a corner of the kitchen, where she had to endure the crude jokes of the male drudges, as the donkey skin made her appear so dirty and disgusting. After a while, however, the novelty wore off. Moreover, the farmer's wife took her under her wing, as the young Princess was so conscientious about her work. She drove the sheep and led the turkeys out to graze with such competence that it seemed as if she had never done anything else. Everything she put her hands to was fruitful.

One day sitting beside a clear spring, where she often lamented her sad situation, she thought to look at her reflection in the water. The horrible donkey skin that covered her like a hairy cape and cowl revolted her. Ashamed of the change that had come over her, she washed her face and her hands, which became whiter than ivory, and her beautiful complexion returned to its natural freshness. The joy of rediscovering her beauty moved her to bathe in the pool. But afterward she had to put on her filthy skin again before she could return to the farm.

Luckily, the next day happened to be a holiday, so she had the time to tap the Fairy's wand to the ground and make the chest appear. And so she freshened up, powdered her lovely hair, and put on the beautiful dress that was the color of the sky, though her room was so small that the train of her dress could not be unfurled. The Princess looked at herself and (with good reason) admired her beauty, so much so that she resolved to take turns putting on her magnificent dresses on holidays and Sundays as a pleasant diversion, which she did regularly. She entwined flowers and diamonds in her hair with tasteful flair, and often she sighed, for she had no witness to her beauty but the sheep and

The joy of rediscovering her beauty moved her to bathe in the pool.

the turkeys, who loved her just as well in the horrible donkey skin—"Donkey-skin" being the name she had been given on the farm.

One feast day, when Donkey-skin had put on her Sun-colored dress, the son of the king to whom the farm belonged came there to rest on his return from the hunt. This Prince was young and handsome, beloved of his father and his mother the queen, and adored by the people. Offered a simple peasant meal, the young Prince accepted, and afterward began to explore the farm, poking his head into every barnyard and hidden corner. Roaming from place to place, he entered a dark alley at the end of which he noticed a closed door. Curiosity made him put his eye to the key-hole—but what must he have thought when he saw a Princess so beautiful and so richly dressed, of so noble and dignified an air that he took her for a divinity? The impetuosity of his feelings at this moment would have led him to break down the door, but for the respect that this ravishing creature inspired in him.

He could barely drag himself away from this dark and obscure alley, except to discover who it was who lived in this little room. He was told that she was a scullery maid called Donkey-skin, due to the animal hide that she always wore, and that she was so dirty and unpleasant that no one spared a glance for her or even spoke to her, and that she had been hired on out of pity, to look after the sheep and the turkeys.

The Prince, unsatisfied with this explanation, saw that these vulgar people knew nothing else and that it was useless to question them. So he returned to the palace of his father the king, more in love than words can say, and everywhere seeing the image of the beautiful goddess he had spied through the keyhole. He regretted not having knocked at the door, and promised himself that he would not miss his chance the next time.

But the turmoil in his heart, caused by the intensity of his love, gave him that night a fever so severe he was soon at death's door. The queen, who had no other child, despaired because every remedy proved useless. She promised the most lavish rewards to the doctors, but all in vain, for though they applied all their skill, nothing could cure the Prince.

At last they concluded that some great sorrow must be the cause of his sickness. They told the queen, who, full of tenderness for her son, went to him and begged him to tell her the cause of his grief; that even if it were a matter of passing the crown down to him, his father would cede the throne to him without regret; or if he desired some princess, even if they were at war with her father and the people justly complained, they would sacrifice it all to obtain what he desired. She implored him not to let himself die, since on his life theirs depended.

The grief-stricken queen did not finish this touching speech without moving the Prince to tears.

"Madam," he said at last, in a very feeble voice, "I am not so debased as to covet my father's crown. May it please heaven that he live for many years, and that he may long have me as the most faithful and most respectful of his subjects. As for the princesses you offer me, I have not yet thought of marrying, and you can rest assured that, subject as I am to your wishes, I will always obey you, no matter what it may cost me."

"Oh! my son," replied the queen, "we will spare nothing to save your life. But, my dear child, save mine and that of your father the king by telling me what you desire, and be assured that you will have it."

"Well, madam," he said, "since you would know my thoughts, I will obey. It would be a crime to endanger two lives so dear to me. It is this, my mother: I want Donkey-skin to make me a cake, and to have it brought to me as soon as it's ready."

The queen, bemused by this strange name, asked who this Donkey-skin was.

"It is, madam," replied one of her officers who had by chance seen her, "the ugliest beast imaginable next to a wolf, with a dark, hairy hide. A filthy scullion who lives on your farm and minds your turkeys."

"It matters not," said the queen. "My son, after returning from the hunt, has perhaps eaten one of her pastries. It is the delirious wish of a dying man. What I am saying is, I want Donkey-skin to make him a cake as soon as possible."

A messenger ran to the farm and relayed the order that Donkey-skin was to make a cake for the Prince as best she could.

Some authors believe that, at the moment the Prince had put his eye to the keyhole, Donkey-skin had noticed it. And then, looking from her little window, she had seen him, so young, so handsome, and so well put together that the memory had caused her more than a few sighs.

Either way—having seen him or having heard him spoken of with praise—Donkey-skin was delighted to be able to become known to him. She shut herself in her little room, threw off the ugly skin, washed her face and hands, arranged her hair, put on a beautiful shiny silver corset and similarly pretty petticoat, and then started to make the much-desired cake. She used the finest flour and the freshest eggs and butter. While working the ingredients, whether on purpose or not, a ring from her finger fell into the batter and got mixed into it. As soon as the cake was finished baking, she swathed herself in her horrible skin and gave the cake to the messenger, asking him for news of the Prince.

But the man, not deigning to answer her, rushed back to the palace to deliver the Prince his cake.

The Prince took the cake eagerly from the man's hands and ate it so voraciously that the doctors present warned that so much haste was not a good sign. Indeed, the Prince thought he might choke on the ring he found in one of the pieces of cake. But he drew it neatly from out of his mouth, and his zeal for devouring the cake was forgotten as he examined the fine emerald set in a ring of gold, a band so dainty that he thought it could only fit on the prettiest finger in the world.

He kissed this ring a thousand times, put it under his mattress, and pulled it out any time he thought no one would see him. The torment that plagued him, as he wondered how he might see the woman who belonged to this ring—not daring to believe that, if he asked for Donkey-skin, she would be allowed to come, and not daring to speak of what he had seen through the keyhole, for fear that he would be laughed at as a fantasist—brought back his fever with a vengeance. The doctors, not knowing what more to do, declared to the queen that the Prince was sick with love, and the desperate queen and the king ran to their son.

"My son, my dear son," cried the grieving king, "tell us the name of the one you desire. We swear that we will bring her to you, even if she is the lowliest of peasants."

Kissing him, the queen agreed with all that the king had said, and the Prince, moved by the tears and caresses of those who gave him life, said to them, "My father and my mother, I in no way desire to make a marriage that displeases you. And as proof of the truth of this," he added, drawing the emerald from under his mattress, "I will marry the one to whom this ring belongs. It is not likely to be that one who owns such a pretty finger is a yokel or a peasant."

The king and the queen took the ring, examined it with curiosity, and judged, like the Prince, that it could only belong to the daughter of a good house. Then the king, having kissed his son and implored him to get better, went out, commanded that the drums and fifes and trumpets be sounded throughout the city, and had the heralds announce that the one whose finger could fit a certain gold ring would marry the heir to the throne.

First the princesses arrived, then the duchesses, and the marquises, and the baronesses—but no matter how small they tried to make their fingers, none could put on the ring. So next came the young women of common birth; but pretty as they all were, their fingers were too fat. The Prince, who was feeling better, tried the rings on the girls himself. Finally, it came down to the chambermaids, but they fared no better. Then, when everyone else had tried, the Prince asked for the cooks, the scullery maids, and the shepherdesses. They were all brought to the palace, but their red, stubby fingers could hardly fit through the ring beyond the nail.

"Are they going to bring in Donkey-skin, who made me the cake?" asked the Prince.

Everyone laughed and said no, she was too dirty and disgusting.

"Let someone find her now," said the king. "It will not be said that I have left anyone out."

His servants ran, doubled over with laughter, mocking the very idea of seeking out the turkey-girl.

The Princess, who had heard the drums and the cries of the heralds, had no doubt that the ring was the cause of this uproar. She loved the Prince, and as true love is timorous and has no vanity, she was in perpetual fear that some other lady would have a finger as small as hers. So she was overjoyed when the king's servants came and knocked on her door. Since she knew that they were seeking the owner of a finger suited to her ring, some impulse had moved her to arrange her hair with great care, and to wear her beautiful silver corset, and her petticoat full of frills and silver lace studded with emeralds. At the first knock, she quickly covered her finery with the donkey skin and opened the door. The servants, unable to restrain themselves from teasing her, told her that the king had asked her to marry his son. They broke into unruly bursts of laughter, which didn't cease as they led her back to the Prince.

When they arrived, even he was astonished at the girl's outfit and dared not believe that it was the same girl he had seen who was so majestic and so beautiful. Sad and confused to be so badly mistaken, he said, "Is it you who lives at the end of that dark alley in the third barnyard of the farm?"

"Yes, my lord," she replied.

"Show me your hand," said the Prince, trembling and heaving a heavy sigh.

Well, now! Weren't the king and queen, their chamberlains, and all the courtiers surprised when, from under that grimy donkey skin, came a delicate little white and pink hand, and the ring slipped easily onto the prettiest little finger in the world. Then, with a small shrug of her shoulders, the skin fell from the Princess and so ravishingly beautiful did she appear that the Prince, weak though he was, dropped to his knees and hugged her so ardently that she blushed. But it was hardly noticed, as the king and queen came to embrace her warmly and to ask her if she would marry their son.

The Princess, bewildered by so much attention and by the love of this handsome young Prince, was about to thank them when the ceiling opened, and the Lilac Fairy descended in a chariot made of her name-sake flowers and branches and, with infinite grace, told them the Princess's story. The king and queen, charmed to see that Donkey-skin was a great Princess, held her doubly tight. But the Prince was even more moved by her virtue, and his love increased as the Fairy recounted her tale.

The Prince's impatience to marry the Princess was such that he barely allowed enough time to make the appropriate preparations for such an illustrious wedding. The king and queen, who were deeply fond of their future daughter-in-law, smothered her with affection. She had declared that she could not marry the Prince without the consent of her father the King. So he was the first to be sent an invitation—without, however, being told the name of the bride. The Lilac Fairy, who presided over everything, as was proper, had advised this little omission to avoid the potentially unpleasant consequences.

Kings from all countries came—some in sedan chairs, others in open carriages, and some who came from the most distant countries rode on elephants and tigers and eagles. But the most magnificent and most glorious of all was the father of the Princess. He had fortunately gotten over his deranged love and had married a very beautiful queen who was a widow. The Princess ran to meet him, and he recognized her at once and embraced her with great tenderness before she had time to throw herself on her knees. The king and queen presented their son to him, whom he welcomed with

Kings from all countries came.

open arms. The wedding took place with all imaginable pomp, but the young couple were hardly aware the ceremony was going on, as they only had eyes for each other.

In spite of the protests of the noble young Prince, his father the king had his son crowned that very day and, kissing his hand, placed him on the throne. The celebrations of this glorious union lasted nearly three months, but the love of these two young people would have endured for more than a hundred years, had they lived that long.

THE ORAL.

Hard to believe as it may sound,
As long as there are children around,
Their grandmas and mamas will ensure
That this Donkey-skin tale will endure.

One day when she was at the fountain, an old woman approached and begged her for a drink.

The Fairies

NCE upon a time there was a widow who had two daughters. The elder resembled her mother so much in appearance and in temper that she was often mistaken for her—both were so disagreeable and arrogant that no one could tolerate either of them. The younger daughter, who was the image of her father in sweetness and kindness, was also one of the most beautiful girls anyone had ever seen.

As we are naturally drawn to those like ourselves, the mother was crazy about her first-born daughter, and at the same time intensely disliked her second daughter. She made the younger girl take her meals in the kitchen and toil from before sunup until after dark. Among other duties, this poor child had to go twice a day to draw water more than a mile away and bring it home in a large jug.

One day when she was at the fountain, an old woman approached and begged her for a drink.

"Yes, of course, my good woman," said this pretty young maid. Rinsing her jug, she drew some water from the clearest part of the fountain and handed it to the old lady, still supporting the pitcher so that she might drink from it more easily.

The good woman, having drunk her fill, said to her, "You are so beautiful, so good and kind that I must present you with something"—for this was in fact a Fairy who had taken the form of an old village crone to judge the kindness of this young girl—"The gift I will give you," the Fairy continued, "is that with every word you utter will fall out of your mouth either a flower or a precious stone."

When the girl arrived back home, her mother scolded her for being so late in coming back from the fountain.

"I beg your pardon, mother," said the poor girl. And as she spoke these words, out of her mouth fell a rose, two pearls, and two large diamonds.

"What's this I see?" asked her mother, astonished. "Do I see pearls and diamonds coming out of her mouth? Where do these come from, my daughter?" (This was the first time she had called her "my daughter.")

The poor child innocently told her everything that had happened at the fountain, all the while scattering diamonds everywhere.

"Really?" said her mother. "I must send my daughter there. Here, Fanchon, look what comes out of your sister's mouth when she speaks! Wouldn't you like to have that gift? You only have to go and get some water at the fountain, and when a poor woman asks you for a drink, give it to her kindly."

"That'd be a fine thing to see," replied the rude girl. "'Go to the fountain'—yeah, sure!"

"I wish for you to go," said her mother, "and go this instant."

So the elder daughter went off, grumbling the whole way. And she'd taken the finest silver flagon in the house. No sooner had she reached the fountain than she saw a splendidly dressed lady emerge from the woods and ask her for a drink. It was the same Fairy who had appeared to her sister as a crone, now disguised as a princess to see how far this girl's rudeness would go.

"You think I came here just to fetch you a drink?" said this graceless snob. "That's right. I brought a silver flagon all the way here especially for you to drink from. Drink from the fountain, if you're so thirsty!"

"You are hardly kind," said the Fairy, with no hint of anger. "Well, since you are so obliging, I give you this as a gift: that for every word you say, a snake or a toad will fall out of your mouth."

When her mother caught sight of her coming back, she cried out, "Well, daughter?"

"Well, what, mother?" replied the rude girl, spewing up a viper and two toads.

"Good heavens!" cried her mother. "What's this I see? Her sister is the cause of this, and she is going to pay!" And immediately she ran off to give her younger child a thrashing.

But the poor girl had fled and hidden in the forest nearby. The king's son, returning from the hunt, encountered her there, and seeing how beautiful she was, asked what she was doing there all alone, and what was making her cry.

"Alas, sir," she cried, "it was my mother who drove me out of the house!"

The prince, seeing six or seven pearls and as many diamonds fall out of her mouth, begged her to tell him where they came from. She recounted her whole adventure for him. The prince fell in love with her, and considering that such a gift was worth more than any dowry, he took her to the palace of the king his father, where they were married.

As for the sister, she became so hateful that finally even her mother chased her out of the house. The unhappy girl, after searching in vain for anyone who was willing to take her in, went off into a corner of the forest to die.

*The king's son, returning from the hunt, encountered her there,
and seeing how beautiful she was, asked what she was doing there
all alone, and what was making her cry.*

THE  MORAL.

Roses, diamonds, and pearls
Can turn heads and may be very nice,
But the sweet words of girls
Have more weight and fetch a higher price.

ANOTHER.

Kindness demands a small cost,
Added to the convenience lost,
But in due course its rewards increase,
Though we tend to think of it least.

Bluebeard

NCE upon a time there was a man who owned beautiful homes in both the city and country, gold and silver place settings, embroidered furnishings, and carriages of gold. But, unfortunately, this man also possessed a blue beard, which made him so ugly that there was not a woman or girl who would not run at the sight of him.

One of his neighbors, a lady of good breeding, had two quite beautiful daughters. He asked for the hand of one in marriage, leaving it to their mother to choose which she would give him. Neither girl wanted him, however, and his offer was thrown back and forth like a hot potato, neither being able to accept a man with a blue beard. What repelled them further was that he had already married several women, and no one knew what had become of them.

Bluebeard, so that they could get to know him better, invited the two girls, along with their mother, three or four of their best friends, and a few young men from the neighborhood, to one of his country houses, where they stayed for a full eight days. Their time there was spent going for walks and at hunting and fishing parties, dances, feasts, and luncheons. They never slept but spent all night in games and playing pranks on one another. In short, everything went so well that the younger daughter began to think that maybe the host's beard wasn't so very blue after all, and that he was a very kind man. As soon as they were back in town, the marriage was arranged and their wedding took place.

At the end of a month, Bluebeard told his new wife that he was obliged to travel to a distant part of the kingdom on important business, a trip that would take at least six weeks. He encouraged her to entertain herself well during his absence, and suggested that she invite some of her friends and take them to the country, if she wished—whatever would make her happy.

"Here," he said, "are the keys for the two large storage rooms, and here is the one that locks up the gold and silver plate, which is not for everyday use. This key belongs to the safes where my gold and silver are kept, this to the chests containing my jewels. And here you have the master key that gives admittance to all the rooms. As for this little key, it is the key to my study at the end of the long corridor on the lower floor. You may open anything, you may go anywhere, but I

"If you happened to unlock this room, I would be so furious that there is no telling what I might do."

forbid you to enter this room. I forbid it absolutely—if you happened to unlock this room, I would be so furious that there is no telling what I might do."

She promised to follow his instructions to the letter. After giving her a kiss good-bye, Bluebeard climbed into his coach and set off on his journey.

The young bride's friends and neighbors did not bother to wait for an invitation, they were so impatient to see the splendors of her new home. They had not dared to visit while her husband was there, for his blue beard frightened them. But there they were now, going through the closets, wardrobes, and bedrooms, each one more magnificent than the last. Then they went upstairs to the store rooms, where they were in awe of the beauty and number of the tapestries, beds, sofas, cabinets, tables, and stands. There were mirrors in which they could see themselves from head to foot, some with frames of glass, others with frames of gilded silver and ruby, the loveliest and finest things they had ever seen. They couldn't stop extolling their friend for her good fortune and envying her happiness. She, however, was less dazzled by all of these riches, as she was itching to go and open the downstairs study.

She was so overcome by curiosity that, without considering how rude it was to leave her guests, she descended a hidden staircase with such haste that she nearly broke her neck two or three times on her way

*The young bride's friends and neighbors were so impatient
to see the splendors of her new home.*

down. Arriving at the door of the study, she hesitated,
remembering the warning her husband had given her
and thinking about what unhappy consequences might
result from disobeying him. But the temptation was too

strong for her to overcome. So she took the small key and, with a trembling hand, opened the study door.

At first she saw nothing, for the windows were closed, but after a few moments she began to realize that the floor was entirely covered and sticky with blood, in which were reflected the bodies of many dead women strung up along the walls. These were all the women Bluebeard had married and whose throats he had cut, one after another.

She thought she would die from fear, and as she drew the key out of the lock, it fell from her hand. When she had regained her senses somewhat, she picked up the key, closed the door, and ran up to her room to try to recover. But it was no use, for she was too shaken by what she'd seen. Noticing that the key of the study was stained with blood, she wiped it two or three times, but the blood would not come off. No matter how much she washed it, and even scrubbed it with sand and grit, the blood always remained—for the key was enchanted, and there was no way to clean it completely. When the blood was removed from one side, it reappeared on the other.

Bluebeard returned from his trip that very evening. He had received some letters along the way, he said, that confirmed that the business he had been on had concluded to his advantage. His wife did everything she could to show him that she was delighted by his prompt return.

The next day he demanded the return of his keys. She gave them to him, but with a hand trembling so noticeably that he easily guessed what had happened.

"How is it," he asked her, "that the key to my study is not with the others?"

"I must have left it upstairs on my table," she said.

"Do not fail to bring it to me this instant," said Bluebeard.

After delaying as long as she could, she had to bring him the key. Bluebeard examined it carefully and said to his wife, "Why is there blood on this key?"

"I know nothing about it," said the poor girl, paler than death.

"You know nothing?" replied Bluebeard. "Well, I *do* know. You wanted to enter my study? Well, madam, you will enter it again, and you will take your place among the ladies you've seen there."

She threw herself at her husband's feet, sobbing and begging forgiveness, with all the signs of true repentance, for having been disobedient. She would have softened a stone, as beautiful and in distress as she was, but Bluebeard had a heart harder than stone.

"You must die, madam," he said, "and right now."

"Since I must die," she said, beseeching him with eyes that were wet with tears, "give me a little time to say my prayers."

"I'll give you a quarter of an hour," replied Bluebeard, "but not a moment longer."

When the poor girl was alone, she called her sister to her and said, "My sister Anne"—for that was her name—"climb up, I beg you, to the top of the tower and see if our brothers are not approaching. They promised that they would come and visit me today. If you see them, make signs for them to hurry."

Her sister Anne climbed to the top of the tower, and the poor desperate girl cried out to her from time to time, "Anne, my sister Anne, do you see anything?"

And her sister Anne replied, "I see nothing but the sun shining and the green grass growing."

Finally, Bluebeard, holding a great cutlass, shouted out at the top of his voice, "Come down here quickly, or I'll come up there!"

"Oh please, one moment more," his wife replied. And at the same moment she cried under her breath, "Anne, my sister Anne, do you see anything?"

And again her sister Anne answered, "I see nothing but the sun shining and the green grass growing."

"Come down here this instant," yelled Bluebeard, "or I will come up there myself!"

"I am coming," said his wife. Then she cried, "Anne, my sister Anne, do you see anything?"

"I see," replied her sister Anne, "a great cloud of dust coming this way."

"Is it our brothers?"

"Alas, no, my sister, it is only a flock of sheep."

"Do you refuse to come down?" Bluebeard roared.

"One moment more!" replied his wife. Once more she cried, "Anne, my sister Anne, do you see anything at all?"

"I see," replied her sister, "two horsemen coming this way, but they are still a long way off." A moment later, she cried, "Heaven be praised! They are our brothers. I am waving at them to hurry as much as I can."

Bluebeard bellowed such a mighty roar that the whole house trembled. His poor wife went downstairs and threw herself at his feet, disheveled and in tears.

"That won't do you any good," Bluebeard said. "You must die."

Then, seizing her by the hair with one hand and with the other lifting the cutlass aloft, he prepared to cut off her head. The poor girl, turning towards him and fixing him with dying eyes, begged for a brief moment more to pray.

"No! no!" he cried. "Commend your soul to Heaven." And raising his arm—

At that moment the door was struck so hard at the gate that Bluebeard stopped short. The gate was opened, and in dashed two horsemen, who drew their swords and rode straight at Bluebeard. He recognized

A moment later, she cried, "Heaven be praised!
They are our brothers."

They plunged their swords into his body.

them as his wife's brothers—one a dragoon, and the other a musketeer—and immediately tried to flee and save himself. But the brothers were so close upon him that they caught him before he could reach the stairs. They plunged their swords into his body, killing him. The poor girl was nearly as stricken as her husband and lacked the strength to rise and embrace her brothers.

It turned out that Bluebeard had no heirs, and that as a result his wife became mistress of all he possessed. She devoted a portion to arranging a marriage between her sister Anne and a young gentleman with whom she had been in love for some time, and another portion to purchase a captain's commission for each of her brothers. The rest formed a dowry for her own marriage with a very good man, who banished from her mind all memory of the horrible time she had spent with Bluebeard.

THE ORAL.

Curiosity, in spite of the merit due it,
So often makes many a woman rue it,
Every day, more examples we see,
It is, to both sexes, a pleasure so slight,
As soon as it's taken, it ceases to be,
And always the price is too high.

ANOTHER.

If you see with sensible eyes,
And are a little bit worldly wise,
You'll know that this tale we put on,
Has come from a long time gone;
No such groom could now live,
Asking what his bride cannot give,
Plagued by misery and jealousy,
Spinning his wife a tale so zealously;
And whether his beard was blue or light gray,
He'd soon find out who is master today.

Jupiter appeared before him, thunderbolt in hand.

The Ridiculous Wishes

Illustrated by Harry Clarke

NCE upon a time there was a poor wood-cutter who, weary of his hard life, said he had a yearning to go and rest on the banks of the Acheron—the river of woe in the underworld—claiming, in his profound sadness, that ever since he had come into this world, cruel Heaven had refused to grant even one of his wishes.

One day when he was in the woods and started complaining, Jupiter appeared before him, thunderbolt in hand. It would be difficult to portray in words the fear that this good man felt. "I want nothing," he said, throwing himself on the ground, "no wishes, no thunder, Lord. Let's consider the score even."

"Quit your cowering," said Jupiter. "I have come, because your lament moved me, to make you see how unfairly you judge me. Listen then: To you I promise, I who am the sovereign master over the whole world, to fulfill completely the first three wishes that you decide to make, no matter what they are. Imagine what could make you happy, what would satisfy you. And, since your happiness depends on your wishes, consider them carefully before you make them."

At these words, Jupiter ascended to the heavens, and the happy woodcutter, hugging his bundle of logs, threw it onto his back to take it home. That burden had never seemed lighter to him.

"It goes without saying," he said, while trotting home, "that I must not do anything lightly. This is an important matter, and I must get my wife's advice."

Arriving home under his fern roof, he greeted his wife. "Fanchon," he said, "let's have a big fire and a feast, my darling. We are going to be rich from now on, and all we need to do is make wishes."

At which point he recounted everything that had happened. Upon hearing this story, his lively, quick-witted wife formed a thousand vast projects in her mind. But, considering the importance of acting prudently, she said to her husband, "Blaise, my dear friend, let's not spoil anything by being impatient. Let's weigh carefully what we ought to do with such a gift. We should put off making a decision on our first wish and sleep on it."

"That's how I see it, too," said her husband Blaise. "But go and draw us some wine from behind the kindling."

When she returned, he drank and, enjoying the sweetness of reclining beside a roaring fire, he said, leaning back in his chair, "With such a good fire going, a yard's length of black pudding would be perfect right now."

He'd hardly finished speaking these words when, to his wife's great astonishment, she caught sight of a very long black pudding that, starting from one corner of the hearth, wriggled like a snake toward her. She immediately cried out. But realizing that this mishap was due to the wish that, out of sheer stupidity, her reckless husband had made, there was no scorn or insult that, in her spite and anger, she did not hurl at her husband.

"When we could have an empire, gold, pearls, rubies, diamonds, fine clothes, was it really necessary to ask for a blood sausage?"

"Very well, I'm in the wrong," he said. "I made a poor choice, I made a huge mistake. I'll do better next time."

"Oh, fine, fine," she said. "Why don't you wait for me under the elm? To make a wish like that, you must be as dumb as an ox!"

Her husband, carried away with anger, more than once considered muttering the wish to be widowed,

*She caught sight of a very long black pudding that
wriggled like a snake toward her.*

and between us, it's possible he could have done worse. "Men," he said, "really have a nose for suffering! Damn the pudding, and damn it again. I wish to God, you cursed shrew, that he would hang it from the end of *your* nose!"

His prayer was immediately answered by Heaven, and as soon as the husband let loose those words, a yard's length of black pudding attached itself to the nose of his irritated wife. This unexpected marvel only angered him further.

Fanchon was a pretty young woman with much grace, and to tell the truth, this new ornament did not exactly complement her beauty. On the other hand, hanging as it did over the lower part of her face and covering her mouth, it did prevent her from speaking easily—such a wonderful advantage to a husband that in that happy moment he considered wishing nothing more.

"To compensate for such a terrible misfortune," he said to himself, "I could very well use the wish I have left to become a king in the blink of an eye. Nothing equals the grandeur of a sovereign, it's true, but I must also think of how my queen would look, and what sorrow it would plunge her into to place her on a throne with a nose longer than a yard. I must listen to her about this and let her make the decision—either to become a great queen while keeping the horrible nose she has, or

*To tell the truth, this new ornament did not exactly
complement her beauty.*

to remain a woodcutter's wife with a nose like anyone else's, as she had before this misfortune."

She carefully thought the matter over. Whatever the power and effect of a scepter might be, or the fact that, when you wear a crown, your nose is always shapely, since there is nothing that does not yield to the desire to please a monarch, she preferred to keep her peasant's babushka rather than be queen and be ugly.

And so the woodcutter did not change his station in life. He did not become a potentate, he did not fill his purse with coins. He was all too happy to use the wish that remained—a feeble happiness, a poor resource— to restore his wife to the way she had been.

THE MORAL.

It is a fact that for men so miserable,
Blind, reckless, anxious, and malleable,
It pays not to convert wishes to truth,
For few of them are remotely capable,
Of putting Heaven's gifts to good use.

147

Charles Perrault.

About the Author

HARLES PERRAULT was born in Paris on January 12, 1628, the seventh child of Pierre Perrault and Paquette Le Clerc. The Perraults were a wealthy bourgeois family, and the father served in the royal government, a career path Charles and some of his brothers would later pursue.

Like his brothers, Charles was sent to the finest schools, attending the Collège de Beauvais beginning at age nine. Having begun writing at an early age and preferring to discover new ways of looking at old texts rather than accepting stock answers (which often irritated his teachers), he was nonetheless at the head of his class. Prior to his last year of school, his tutor encouraged him to write a thesis. But when his parents declined to pay for this, his tutor took out his disappointment on young Charles, who subsequently opted to stop going to classes and pursue his study of the classics together with another schoolmate who had suffered similar ostracism. Together for the next three or four years, they studied ancient philosophy at home, reading the Bible,

Vergil, and Horace by day and strolling the Luxembourg Gardens in the late afternoons to talk about what they'd learned. These events, from his posthumously published memoirs, would presage his independent approach to scholarship and practice for the rest of his life.

Though he was admitted to the bar in 1651, he quickly wearied of the law after trying only two cases and in 1654 accepted a position as clerk under his older brother Pierre, who was the receiver-general (tax collector) of Paris. Charles stayed in this office for ten years, spending his spare time writing poetry and overseeing the construction of his brother's house in 1657. The skill he showed in this project prompted Louis XIV's finance minister Jean Baptiste Colbert to bring him on as his secretary at the Académie des Inscriptions et Belles-Lettres in 1663, where Charles worked in the superintendence of royal buildings. When a new section of the Louvre was being planned, Charles was able to get his brother Claude appointed to the small council of three overseeing it and suggested the Colonnade, which was built between 1667 and 1674.

In 1668 Perrault wrote *La Peinture* (*Painting*) a poem in honor of Charles Le Brun, Louis XIV's painter, and in 1671 he was elected to the Académie Française. In 1669 he advised Louis XIV to add thirty-nine fountains to the planned labyrinth in the Gardens of Versailles, each fountain depicting one of Æsop's fables. The creation and installation of the animal sculptures, which featured jets of water spurting from their mouths was begun in 1672, the same year Perrault married nineteen-year-old Marie Guichon.

Plan of the Labyrinth at Versailles.

Perrault also had an illustrated guidebook, *Labyrinte de Versailles*, printed at the royal press in 1677. Unfortunately, his whimsical and immensely popular creation lasted little more than a century, as Louis XVI, in one of the lesser missteps of his reign, had the labyrinth destroyed in order to make way for an English garden stocked with exotic trees.

Around the same time, Perrault became involved in one of the more heated intellectual debates of the century, the so-called Quarrel of the Ancients and Moderns. After Jean-Baptiste Lully's and Philippe Quinault's opera *Alceste* was denounced by traditionalists for deviating from classical theater, Perrault wrote a defense of the relatively new form of musical theater titled *Critique de l'Opéra* (1674), which declared the work better than its source material, the classical tragedy *Alcestis* by Euripides. This debate, which Perrault's treatise instigated, continued with his eager participation well into the 1680s, after Perrault was forced into retirement at the age of fifty-six in 1682. He wrote *The Century of Louis the Great* (1687) and *Parallel between Ancients and Moderns* (1688–92), where he argued the superiority of the literature of the seventeenth century.

The Ancients, led by Racine and Boileau, maintained that no writer could surpass the authors of antiquity, that the best they could do was to simply imitate them. The Moderns, led by Perrault, Fontenelle, and Marivaux, argued that new scholarship and new innovations allowed modern men to create new and better forms than the ancients could have imagined. The debate was a proxy of sorts for the larger argument over conservative versus progressive values that continues to this day.

Perrault and his wife Marie had four children before her untimely death after the birth of their youngest, Pierre, in 1678. As the widower father of four children under the age of six, Perrault no doubt practiced refining the folktales of Mother Goose on them, continuing the ages-old oral tradition of sharing and revising the tales, before setting down new versions of them in print sixteen years later.

In retirement Perrault also started to write epic poetry, including a poem on the life of St. Paulinus of Nola in 1686, but it was in revising Boccaccio's tale about Griselda that

Perrault caught the germ of an idea that would make him immortal. Too long and lacking in any sort of magical element, "Grisélidis" was closely related to the kind of tale Perrault would soon become identified with. "The Ridiculous Wishes" and "Donkey-Skin," two fairy tales in verse, followed, published separately and then with the former in the book *Grisélidis*. These led next to the 1695 hand-drawn manuscript *Tales of Mother Goose* and his landmark book, *Stories or Tales of Times Past: With Morals*, in 1697. Originally attributed to his youngest son, Pierre Darmancour (who took the name from a property his father had bought for him), there has never been much doubt that Charles actually wrote them. (It has been plausibly suggested, however, that Pierre wrote a first draft that his father substantially edited. At only twenty-two years of age, Pierre died in 1700 while serving as a lieutenant in the French Army.)

After the massive success of his *Stories or Tales of Times Past*, Perrault wrote another major pro-Modern book between 1696 and 1700, entitled *The Illustrious Men Who Have Appeared in France During This Century*, and in 1699 he translated the *One Hundred Fables* (*Fabulae Centum*) of the Italian poet Gabriele Faerno from Latin into French verse. In 1702 he completed his memoirs, though they would not be published until 1909. Charles Perrault continued writing and publishing up until his death at the age of seventy-five on May 16, 1703.

For a self-professed and committed Modern, Perrault's name has become as esteemed as one of the ancients his opponents idolized. And his fame and longevity derive from his retelling of tales more ancient than the classics. And yet, despite the apparent irony, Perrault exemplified the Modern approach he championed by making these dusty old tales new, daring to improve on stories handed down from mothers and grandmothers to children since before Vergil or Homer were old enough to hold a quill. He took a traditional form with no respect for logic—filled with magic, mania, madness, and mayhem—kept the wonder and horror, and introduced reason with a healthy dose of ironic self-awareness.

The folklorist Andrew Lang, in *Perrault's Popular Tales* (1888), called him "a born Irregular…a truant from school, a deserter of the Bar, an architect without professional training, a man of letters by inclination, a rebel against the tyranny of the classics, and immortal by a kind of accident." And author Angela Carter wrote of Perrault in the afterword to her 1977 translation, *Little Red Riding-Hood, Cinderella, and Other Classic Fairy Tales of Charles Perrault,* that he was "a man who wanted to make of Paris a modern Rome, a visible capital of sweet reason, and his fairy tales are in a style…marked by precision of language, irony, and realism." In creating his new classics, Perrault also ushered in a new age of retellings and reimaginings. And authors from every place and every era since have used his example to make these and countless other tales new by making them their own.

CPSIA information can be obtained
at www.ICGtesting.com
Printed in the USA
BVHW032042290720
584854BV00019B/39